Fight for Me

Hannah Martinez

Published by Hannah Martinez, 2023.

FIGHT FOR ME

First edition. May 30, 2023.

ISBN: 979-8215658130

Written by Hannah Martinez.

Table of Contents

For A.

Thank you for always believing in me

To my M.

Thank you for your love and patience

PROLOGUE

Jenny – 14 years old

I move through the school hallway, passing over wandering students, careful not to run into anyone. Loud music is blaring through my headphones, and I heave a sigh of relief as I exit the building. However, that feeling is short-lived when I sense a little tap on my shoulder. For a second, I consider ignoring it, but it's not like I'm in a rush to get home.

Without removing my headphones, I turn my head to the side and am not surprised to find the new girl, Claire, standing close, her weight shifting from side to side as she nervously bites her lip. She starts to babble something, gesturing wildly with her hands, almost smacking me in the face in the process. Then she waits for my answer with a hopeful expression on her face.

Trying to look bored, I slowly get one of my headphones out and ask, "Did you say something?"

Not looking even slightly deterred by my rude behavior, Claire repeats as if rehearsed, "Hi, Jenny. I'm sorry to bother you again. But I heard about a party happening today at the Mill, and I wondered if you could take me with you. Of course, assuming you are going."

"I am," I respond noncommittally, as I am already putting the earpiece back into my ear and turning to walk away. Before I can take even two steps, I feel another tap on my shoulder. With a sigh, I look up to the heavens. *God, give me patience.*

The Mill is what we call an abandoned place on the outskirts of Bell Ridge, a small town my family moved to after my father was discharged from the army. The place used to be a farm belonging to Old Man Sturgis, who was a mean, old fart. But after he moved to Florida to retire, the place got turned into a party spot for horny teenagers and a safe space for questionable characters to enjoy their illegal activities.

I have no idea why everyone is calling it the Mill, as there's no fucking mill on-site, but whatever. The point is, I have no clue why a girl like Claire even wants to go there with me. It's a dump.

I go there almost every Friday, sure, but I'm not what people would call a respectable kind of girl.

Beautiful little girls like Claire never want to be anywhere near me, however, since she moved here from fuck-knows-where, the girl made it her mission to befriend me. She spotted me last week on the first day of school, while I was eating my lunch alone in blissful silence. I don't know what gave her the indication that I would like some company, what's with me wearing the usual "don't fuck with me" mask on my face, but she decided to join anyway.

Even though I didn't show any signs of being interested in making her my new best friend, she started to follow me around like a puppy after that.

What irritates me the most is the fact that I'm starting to find her presence oddly comforting, and I hate getting comfortable around people. That's when the ugly side of them unveils, and that's when they can strike out. Better to keep my guard up.

With that in mind, I stop again and this time Claire goes around me, blocking my way. She looks up at me with an eager smile, and I remove both of my headphones before crossing my

2

arms. I give her a hard stare, hoping for her to run, but she only stares back at me, unblinking.

Jesus Christ, she's impossible.

When her intense stare starts to freak me out a little bit, despite myself, I break and finally ask, "Why do you even want to go to the Mill? The place is terrible, and I'm not good at babysitting."

She laughs, like I'm hilarious, and replies with questions of her own. "Why wouldn't I go? You're going. And a babysitter? We're the same age, dummy."

"Maybe so. But it isn't exactly a place for a girl like you."

"A girl like me?" Claire asks, genuinely confused, with a hand on her chest.

I scoff and put my hands on my hips. "Oh, come on. For one, you're sweet and nice, so I'm sure you wouldn't want to be seen with a mean skank like me in a place like that. Maybe go find some cute little friends, I don't know, in a library or something, and leave me be."

"So you think I'm sweet?" She grins adoringly as she rests her chin on her clasped hands, thoroughly ignoring the part where I said to leave me alone.

"Where the fuck did you come from? I've never met a person like you." I mutter in disbelief, but feel my lips twitching a little with an involuntary smile.

"I'm originally from Riverwalk, Alaska. I was actually homeschooled before moving here. Can you believe it?" She doesn't even wait for an answer as she continues in a conversational tone, her head tilting to the side. "And I don't think you're mean or a skank. I think you are sad and lonely.

3

Most times I feel sad and lonely too, so the moment I saw you I thought we could be less miserable together."

"You? Miserable?" I snort mockingly and try to hide how uncomfortable Claire's personal assessment made me.

"You better believe it. This is just one of my faces." Claire gestures at her overly happy, borderline creepy, smile. "I've got others hidden but if we become friends, I can show you more," she whispers conspiratorially.

My mouth hangs right open, when she backs away from me, her friendly smile back in place. "So, what time will you pick me up?"

I scratch at my neck, completely at a loss. "Shit. Fine. I guess, give me your number and I will text you the details."

All of a sudden, a loud shriek almost bursts my eardrum as two surprisingly strong little arms squeeze my middle, making me almost scream in agony as Claire unknowingly puts pressure on my bruised back. I wince, but quickly compose myself when I notice that we have eyes on us from people still hanging around the parking lot in front of our school. I quickly pat Claire on the back and then remove her arms from around me.

"Rule number one, Claire. If you really want to be friends with me and go places together – keep your hands to yourself."

She throws her hands up in a sorry gesture and backs away. "Sure thing, Jenny."

I shake my head with a sigh and take my phone out of my back pocket. "Give me your number then."

Claire recites it giddily, bouncing on her feet like a child who's about to go on her first ride at an amusement park. After I install her number on my phone under the name "weird girl",

4

I measure her with an unimpressed look. "Rule number two – curb your enthusiasm and keep it cool. There's only so much of your energy I can take on a daily basis."

Claire stops her bouncing at once and with a fake uninterested face looks at her nails and shrugs. "Yeah, sure, I can be cool."

I snort and move around her before throwing off my shoulder, "See ya later, weird girl!"

"Bye, bestie!" She yells after me and causes everyone to look in my direction as I walk away.

I turn back the music on my headphones and cover the distance from school to my street in no time. The whole way, I've been fantasizing about what my life would look like if I had someone fighting in the same corner as me. Someone I could depend on. Someone I could trust.

Could Claire be that person?

The fantasy ends abruptly when I reach my house and see that damn car in the driveway. A sense of doom envelops me, making me lose that extra bounce in my step.

There's no way someone could carry all that burden with me. It's too heavy, and no one deserves to be touched by my shitty life.

But maybe I could keep a friend like Claire, and still keep the shit from spilling out.

Yes, that's what I'll do.

CHAPTER I

J enny – 16 years old

A silent thank-you leaves my lips when I see there's no police car parked in front of my house. My home is completely silent as I enter, so I drop my backpack on my bed and go through the back into the garden, knowing I will probably find my mom working on her flowerbeds.

I spot her kneeling between gardenias, digging in the dirt with her bare hands. She's half-turned toward me, so I don't see her face fully, but I can assume what she's hiding under the big straw hat and giant sunglasses.

The sounds of breaking glass and her whines still resonate in my brain from this morning's fight taking place in our kitchen. Some people would probably call me a coward for it, but I slipped through the back door before my father noticed my presence – I already missed enough school because of that asshole. There will be other opportunities for him to get his frustrations out on me.

When the gravel crunches under my feet, my mom flinches slightly, but relaxes when she sees that it's only me approaching her.

She graces me with a smile and motions for me to join her.

"Hi Jenny, how was school?"

I kneel in the dirt next to her and start weeding. The smell of fresh soil instantly brings me comfort. "School was a stupid waste of time, as usual. But Claire and I started to hang out with a new group of people, so you could say I'm making new friends."

"Oh, please do tell me more. Does there happen to be a boy that you like in said group?" my mom teases.

I scoff and roll my eyes at her. "Boys are fucking useless. They're only good for one thing."

"First of all, language. And second of all, that's not true. I'm sure one day you'll meet a nice young man. Just like I met your father," she replies with a dreamy sigh.

"Like hell I am," I respond sarcastically, not even commenting on how delusional my mother always is when it comes to her husband.

We work in silence for some time, and when I can feel my mother's eyes on me, I look at her quizzically.

"Jenny, you should probably go clean up before David gets home. I don't know what mood he'll be in. We had a disagreement this morning and I wouldn't want you to get in his way," Mom states matter-of-factly and in moments like this, I hate her even more than him.

I nod and after giving her a barely there kiss on her tender cheek, I get up and get in the house. After helping around the garden, I'm all sweaty and feel my stomach rumbling, notifying me of how unhappy it is with me forgetting to eat again. I take a quick shower and then make a sandwich, listening for the approaching car the whole time.

When I'm safely hidden in my room behind locked doors, I finally relax on my bed and grab a book to pass the time.

• • • •

AT SOME POINT, I MUST'VE nodded off because I startle suddenly when I hear rhythmic tapping on my window. The sun is already setting, the beams creating moving shadows in my room. I grab my phone and am surprised when I see it's almost seven. My attention shifts back to the window as the tapping continues. When I get up, my mattress squeaks loudly, and I freeze glancing at my door, but when I don't hear any movements in the house, I rush to check it out.

I curse when I see Claire's eager face plastered to my window.

"Bitch, what the fuck? You know, I'm not allowed any guests," I hiss as I open the window.

Claire climbs through the gap and gracefully lands on the carpet, no sound made.

"Calm down, Jenny. You said yourself that your stuck-up daddy never comes to check on you. And I just saw him pull away, so don't get your panties in a twist," she mutters.

"I don't..." I scratch my forehead and breath out, trying to calm my racing heart. "You should've called, is all. You surprised me."

"Well, I did try calling you when I was close to your house. You didn't pick up, so when I saw your dad driving away, I decided to see what was taking you so long." Claire throws her hands up, like she's got enough of my bullshit. "I don't understand why it's always such a big deal about me coming here anyway. Our dads know each other and on paper I'm the one being reputable out of us two. So, it should be my dad worrying about hanging out with you. Not the other way around."

"Fuck off. And don't come here unannounced again, I could get grounded again," I say faking annoyance, when in reality Claire just scared the shit out of me.

Claire jumps on my bed and crosses her arms. "Fine. Jesus. Can you get a move on now? We were supposed to be there thirty minutes ago. You wouldn't want to keep Marcus waiting," she teases and wiggles her eyebrows.

I scoff but turn around to reach into my closet. "Marcus can wait. I don't give a damn, honestly. I just hope he got us some weed."

"You still haven't told me what happened last week when you two went upstairs."

"What do you think happened?" I mutter distractedly as I take out one of my long-sleeved shirts from the closet. "We talked a bit, and then we fucked."

Claire snorts from behind me. "Shit, Jenny. First, you lose your virginity to..." She snaps her fingers, trying to remember.

I glance at her and throw, "Derek?"

"Yes! Derek, whatever. And now you're sleeping with guys after talking for five minutes?"

I shrug, not really bothered by it. Like I said before, those dumbasses are only good for one thing.

"So, what? I've been called a slut even before I touched a guy in my life. Might as well live up to it. And Marcus is nice on the eyes, polite and can provide me with the good stuff. What's the big deal?"

Claire hums in her throat but doesn't answer as I change into the new set of clothes.

I glance critically at my reflection and sigh. I'm probably not the ugliest person in the world, but I'm far from good-looking. I'm tall for a girl and skinny as all hell with untamable frizzy dark brown hair always flowing wildly around my head. My big eyes complete my whole appearance, overall making me look like a malnourished scarecrow. But I guess my weirdness is not off-putting to most of the idiots at school, since I never had a problem finding someone interested.

Giving up on taming my hair and not bothering with makeup, I quickly put on my tennis shoes before jumping on the bed next to Claire, who looks troubled.

"Are you really that disgusted with me? If you're embarrassed to be my friend, I can be more discreet. Or I could even stop seeing those guys. I don't really care about them, Claire..."

She shakes her head and concentrates on me. "What happened to your back?"

"What?" I ask, caught completely off guard and then make big eyes at Claire, when I realize I just changed in front of her and completely forgot about the bruises marring my shoulder blades. How could I be so fucking careless?

I try to swallow down my panic when Claire takes a hold of my hand. "Babe, is someone hurting you?" When I automatically shake my head in negation, she adds forcefully, "You know, you can tell me, Jenny. I won't judge you."

Still shaking my head, I laugh awkwardly and try to play it off with a wave of my hand. "No! I mean, thanks for the concern, Claire, but I totally forgot about slipping and falling on the track today during the P.E. class. I'm fine though."

She eyes me suspiciously and bites the inside of her cheek, but after looking into my eyes for what feels like an eternity, she nods. "All right, if you say so..."

"That's what happened," I press. "So, are we going or what?" I pull up Claire with me as I stand up.

"Yeah, come on."

· · · ·

WHEN WE REACH THE MILL, the party is already in full swing, and it's completely dark out. The place is crawling with drunk idiots and half-naked girls shaking their asses to some horrible bouncy music that I could only describe as torture. Still, I act as if this is exactly the place I want to be on a Friday night. I grab at Claire's hand, so we don't get separated in the sea of strangers, and drag her toward the familiar group I got a glimpse of in the crowd.

From that point on, everything goes on as usual: we sit around, smoke pot, talk about dumb stuff, and I refrain from rolling my eyes listening to the moronic pick-up lines that Claire has to put up with from every male in the group.

The upside of letting Marcus follow me around is that at least I have a break from those horny vultures, who would say just about anything to get a girl.

The downside is that I have to smile and pretend to listen to him, knowing that he doesn't give a damn about my personality, and that he's just waiting for the moment when I spread my legs for him. This pretense is terribly tiring. Fortunately, Marcus is always eager to share the goods at Friday parties. In general, I'm not a fan of alcohol or drugs, but I'll never deny myself some pot. It makes the company surrounding me seem less annoying, and I even feel like I'm having a good time.

However, after an hour or so, I feel a change in the atmosphere. Something is off. When I look around, I notice it's not just the usual crowd of high school students milling around like before. There's a group of bikers I have never seen around here, and I swear some are wearing some kind of gang symbols. I could be wrong, though. It's Bell Ridge, not Miami, after all.

Looking around, I notice I'm not the only one feeling uneasy with the newcomers. There's a visible gap between the teens and the dangerous-looking men. People cast intrigued or worried glances around and talk in hushed voices.

"Hey, what got you so spooked?" Marcus leans over with an easy smile and nudges my leg with his.

Still eyeing the older men, I respond with a nod in their direction, "What's up with those guys? I've never seen them before. They're giving me the creeps."

Marcus looks up in the direction of the men and shrugs, but there's a small frown between his eyebrows. "Who cares? They're just chilling." He nudges my leg once again to get my attention and when I peer at him with lifted eyebrows, he smiles suggestively, before tilting his head in the direction of the house.

I make eye contact with Claire, who's already watching me like a hawk. When I gesture with my hand where I'm going, she nods and then shows me a thumb down, indicating that she gets where I'm going, and she doesn't approve. Well, that's her problem.

I smile at Marcus and grab his extended hand before we both march into the abandoned building.

• • • •

"ARE YOU STAYING AT the party or heading home? I could give you a ride," Marcus offers as he lightens a cigarette. I pluck it out of his mouth and take a drag before returning it.

"Thanks, but no, thanks. I have to find Claire," I say distractedly as I slip on my jacket and move to unlock the door.

"No goodbye kiss?" Marcus calls after me, but I don't bother answering as I exit in a haste.

This moment after sex is the worst. For me, it's only about physicality and making myself feel good. About my body experiencing positive touch. Staying after seems very intimate, and I don't think I can open up to someone enough for them to look at my naked body full of unwanted marks and imperfections. Maybe I just don't want that with Marcus. I don't know. What I do know is that I always have to flee, or I'll start to freak out.

I almost reach the first step of the staircase when I hear someone downstairs yelling "Cops!" before the music stops abruptly and a stampede of running feet echoes through the building.

"Fuck!" I whisper as I start to descend hurriedly, taking two steps at a time. I pass by a window and try to search for Claire, but it's too dark out to make out anything apart from some moving silhouettes.

I'm running through the corridors trying to get to the backdoor when I'm halted by a loud voice, "Jennifer?"

I whirl around and see the sheriff standing in a big room to my left, surrounded by officers wandering around and trying to wake those who were too wasted to run from the police. The expression my father wears is stricken as he summons me with a wave of his hand.

Real fear washes over me, squeezing me by the throat, and making me feel like I'm drowning when my eyes meet his cold ones. The malicious glint in my father's eyes is promising me punishment in the near future. But not yet. Now we both have a role to play, and it's a well-rehearsed one. We've been here many times. Our masks are now so well crafted, that sometimes even I feel like clapping in astonishment at my father's acting skills.

"Oh, hi Dad. I know this looks bad, but I wasn't drinking, I swear. I only came here with a few of my trusted friends. Please don't be mad." I babble and bite my lip anxiously.

My father sighs heavily, as if he's truly disappointed in me. "Jennifer, you're going to be the death of me, I swear. What are you doing? Your mother was sick with worry. Did you think about that? Now, I will have to tell her you're sneaking out again. And to a place like this one at that." He shakes his head with a frown, and motions around the house.

"No, please don't tell Mom," I whine. "She'll be lecturing me for a month straight again. Pleeease." As I come closer, I clasp my hands in a begging gesture and bat my eyelashes at him with the smile of an angel.

My father puts his hands on his hips and frowns as if he's considering it, when in reality he's probably fantasizing about all the ways he can make me suffer.

One of Dad's officers, I think his name is Rick, steps forward and claps him on the back with an amused expression. "Come on, Sheriff, don't be too hard on your girl. I can't count all the times my kids went behind my back when they were teenagers, it comes with the stupid age. And it doesn't look like she's been drinking."

I smile with a hopeful expression at the man and then focus back on my father. "Yeah, Dad. I promise it won't happen again. I was being stupid. I'll apologize to Mom for scaring her."

15

My dad tilts his head, pretending to battle with himself on how to parent me properly. Man, he's good at this. Sometimes, even I'm convinced that we're normal.

The officer speaks again. "Tell you what, boss. You drive your daughter home, so you can make sure she's safe, and the rest of the guys and I will wrap it up here."

After a short dramatic pause, my father agrees and commands how to proceed to the uniformed men, then grabs me by the shoulder. "Come on, we can continue this conversation at home, young lady."

He steers me to the door and then straight to his car, his grip getting tighter with each step to the point of pain, but I reign in my wince and relax my posture.

When I get in the passenger seat, I quickly take out my phone and text Claire.

Hey, it's me. Did you get away from the cops? Where r u?

My father gets behind the wheel and slams his door, making the car shake, but I don't lift my head from the phone screen, swallowing nervously. I know I'm safe until we reach the house because the sheriff wouldn't risk someone seeing or hearing something they shouldn't. So, I use the time I have to worry about my friend.

My phone pings with a message and I exhale in relief when I read it.

One of the guys drove me home after the police showed up. Don't worry, I'm safe.

Before I get to reply, another text comes through.

Can I come over? We need to talk.

Shit, what is up with her lately? I quickly respond before Claire gets any ideas.

Claire, no! Don't come over, I got busted. They're probably gonna ground my ass. I'll text you tomorrow.

I silence my phone and tuck it safely into my backpack as we park in the driveway. As soon as the car stops, I get out and head to the house. My father walks behind me, breathing down my neck like an angry bull.

No sooner than the doors close behind us when I feel a hand snatching me by the hair and dragging me to a living room before slamming my face hard into the small coffee table. I cry out in pain and my sight gets blurry for a second. I turn, trying to get out of the way of the next oncoming blow, but my movements are too sluggish after the first hit. A giant fist lands in my mid-section, making me wheeze and fall to my knees. I hear hurried footsteps before my mother runs into the room, tears already streaming down her face. When she catches sight of me, she gasps loudly and steps closer. I shake my head for her to not get involved. She hesitates just for a fraction of a second, but when my father slaps me, she covers her mouth with her hands and quickly moves out of the way, cowering in the corner.

I try to move again but this time a sharp kick throws me off my balance and I roll between the table and the couch squealing in pain.

"This is what I fucking fight for, huh? This is what I have to get back to after risking my life each day?! A fucking useless wife and a whore of a daughter spreading her legs for some drug dealers in a fucking dump!" My father roars above me, his spittle raining down on my face.

He bends over my trembling form and grabs my face in one of his hands, his fingers digging into my cheeks, making me flinch.

"Do you have any idea how much you fucking embarrass me with each one of your stunts? Do you want me to turn into a fucking laughingstock at the station? Is that it?"

"No, sir," I try to say, but it comes out muffled because of my father's grip.

He shoves my face away as if touching me is disgusting, and then spits on me before getting up from the floor. "You are a fucking disgrace. Go wash your fucking face and don't let me see you looking like shit again."

My father turns away only to realize that my mother is here in the room with us. He starts toward her with a clenched fist and when she shrinks away with a cry, he stops his flying hand right in front of her face, not making contact, and laughs with contempt.

"Look at the fucking both of you." Dad glances at me as I scramble shakily to my feet, and then focuses on his wife again. "Like mother, like daughter. You're both fucking pathetic. Both always behave like ungrateful whores. You better clean everything up, Marissa." He then kisses my mom on the cheek almost fondly and leaves the room as if he doesn't have a care in the world.

My mom continues to cry, but I ignore her as she tries to straighten everything in the living room with shaking hands. I do as I was told and head straight to the bathroom, hissing when I turn on the light and am greeted by my reflection. My hair is mussed, making me look like I lost a fight with an electric socket. A giant bruise already starts forming on my forehead where my head met the table, and a smeared trickle of blood runs from my split lip. I don't even bother with lifting my shirt up, already knowing sitting straight at school will be a bitch.

I have no idea how long I stay in there, but when I step out of the bathroom, the house is already dark and silent. Without turning the lights on, I move through the hallway in a desperate need of water, but draw to a halt when the sound of a doorbell resonates through the walls.

I see the light switching on in my parents' bedroom and in a panic, I dive into the closest room, which is the kitchen, to take cover. My father marches to the door grumbling threats under his nose, but as soon as the doors open I can hear his tone changing to a politely surprised one.

"Officer Owens? What do I owe the pleasure? It's quite late. Is everything all right at the station?"

I hear a man clearing his throat before an uncertain voice replies. "Sheriff Wallace, I thought this was your address. I'm sorry to bother you so late, sir, but we got a call from a concerned neighbor about some disturbing noises coming out of your house."

I'm so surprised that someone called the police that I chance a peek into the hallway to see what's going on. My father stands in a relaxed pose in front of two police officers. I get a clear view of the one standing closer, but the other one stays in the shadow, a large silhouette towering over the two other men. And my father is not a short guy by any means.

My dad scratches his cheek in puzzlement. "After I came back from the Sturgis' farm with my daughter, we went to sleep. I honestly haven't heard anything happening in the neighborhood. Who placed the call?"

"We don't know, they didn't leave any kind of information. Probably a stupid prank or something. I'm sorry we disturbed you, sir. We'll be on our way."

"It's good that you checked the call, Owens. Better safe than sorry. Now, if that's all, gentlemen."

My father makes a move to close the door, but before he gets the chance, the other person steps into the light and asks in a deep masculine voice, looking straight at me. "Miss, are you all right?"

I jump in surprise that I'm being called out, and then my jaw immediately drops because right there at my front door stands the biggest and most handsome man I've ever seen. He looks like a combination of the Terminator and a GQ model. Hot damn. I don't know if I should be scared or awed.

The deceivingly sweet voice of my father snaps me out of my daze, reminding me of the seriousness of my predicament.

"Jennifer, honey, why aren't you sleeping?" My father's eyes are like lasers in the half-lit corridor, completely at odds with his nice smile.

Shit. Not only was I eavesdropping, but I also showed my busted face to someone. Police officers at that. And here I am staring at some stranger like a complete idiot as my father is probably just plotting the easiest way to bury my body in the backyard. How hard did my head hit the table? Maybe I have a concussion.

"I'm sorry, Dad, I was just getting some water before bed," I say meekly and start to back away.

The big man stops me from leaving when he presses with concern. "Miss, what happened to your face?"

"Oh. This? I'm clumsy. It's nothing," I respond immediately, waving my hand in a dismissive gesture as if it's a small inconvenience happening to all of us daily. But the man's gaze drills into me, straight through my eyes and right into my soul. His expression tells me that he's not fooled.

"Yeah, that's my daughter, all right. Always gets into some messy situations and hurts herself in the process," my father chirps with a jovial smile, but I can tell he doesn't like the man questioning him and paying attention to me.

"Now, I didn't catch your name, officer...?"

"Brody, sir. I'm new in town." The big guy tears his eyes away, and I can finally take a deep breath.

"Oh, yeah, our newest asset. The ex-Marine, right?" my father questions.

"Yes, sir," he responds and then tries again. "May I have a word with your daughter, sheriff? Just to make sure everything is fine."

This time, my father doesn't hide his sneer behind a smile. "You definitely may not." When both officers lift their eyebrows at the sudden change in their boss's demeanor, he schools his features and changes his tone to a more professional one. "Look, Officer Brody. I appreciate your concern and wanting to do everything by the book, but I will not be undermined by some newbie trying to prove himself at my own damn house. You will soon learn how things work around here, but until then, keep in line and stay out of my way. Do you understand me?"

I can say that Brody wants to snap back at my father by the way he stares at him, breathing through his nose harshly, but after the one named Owens jabs him with an elbow, he steps back, and I know it's my cue to get the fuck out of here.

I turn around and hear him rumble, "I'm sorry, sir. I was just trying to do my job. We will be on our way now. Good night."

I don't wait to hear what else is being said as I run back into my room and lock it. My ass hits the floor when my shaking legs stop working. What the fuck was that? No one has ever called the police on my father. Ever. He's the goddamn sheriff.

"Did they arrest him?" A quiet voice reaches me from somewhere in my room, and I muffle a scream with my hand before it alerts my father.

Jumping up to my feet, I go to switch on my bedside lamp and then gawk at my best friend sitting on the bed, still dressed in the outfit she had on at the party.

"Claire?! What the fuck! I almost fucking peed myself!" I whisper-yell at my unwanted guest.

"So that's what you're hiding? It's so much worse than I thought, Jenny. I came here to talk and slipped through the window. And then I heard... I called the police for you. Did they arrest him?" Claire asks with tears in her eyes, her face full of innocent hope.

Oh my God. It was Claire. Of course, it was. I tug my hair in frustration and sit down on the bed next to her.

"I thought you said you were back at your house. How did you get here so fast?"

"Um, I lied. I was already on my way over when I texted." She cringes and lifts her shoulders in a shrug.

"Oh."

"You're not mad, are you? I was trying to help. The police should lock your father away for the whole eternity. I swear I would gladly cut his throat in his sleep," Claire spits vengefully.

"Claire." I sigh. "My father is the sheriff. It's not so easy to get rid of him. They probably wouldn't do anything because they are scared for their jobs. And I would happily watch you cut his throat, but I don't think either of us would be good at disposing of a body."

"What about your mom then? Can't she leave him and take you away?"

"I don't think she's capable of that, to be honest. I used to dream about it and hoped so much for her to finally stand up and say that she's had enough. It never happened," I reply sadly.

"Oh," Claire whispers with a broken expression as she hangs her head.

"Yeah. Oh." I throw my arm around her. "I'm sorry you had to find out this way."

"I had my suspicions for a while. But you were always so evasive and downright convincing that I thought maybe I was reading too much into things." She tilts her head to look at me, with one single tear rolling down her sorrowful face. "I wish that was just one of the times when my mind plays tricks on me. But now that I know, we can think of something together."

"Claire, you finding out doesn't change anything. Today doesn't change anything. This is just how things work in my house."

My best friend removes herself from my embrace, looking thoroughly outraged. "How the fuck can you say that? We have to do something!"

"Like what?" I ask tiredly, feeling overwhelmed by her presence. In moments like this, I wish I were alone like before I met Claire. I wouldn't have to explain anything or have someone stick their nose in things they don't understand.

"I don't fucking know yet! But things are going to change. You'll see."

"Okay, whatever." I sigh and recline on the bed. "If that's all... I'm exhausted and sore, Claire. Can we talk about it some other time?"

"Bitch," Claire whispers and starts to undress.

I sit back up and look up at her, confused. "What are you doing?"

"Staying the night. Duh. Scoot over." She waves her hand, and I move to make room for her in my narrow bed.

I open my mouth to say something, but before I can, Claire lies next to me and whispers, "Sleep, Jenny. We'll talk tomorrow. Tonight I'm keeping an eye on you. You're safe."

I feel the oncoming tears, so before I start bawling like a baby in my best friend's arms, I close my eyes and relax. She grabs my hand and squeezes it once.

With a sigh, I let the fatigue drag me under into nothingness.

CHAPTER II

J enny- 17 years old

It's early spring as I lean on the wall next to the dumpsters behind the school, smoking a cigarette. I shiver slightly as the chilly wind picks up, and I try to shrink into my leather jacket as I'm only half listening to Claire's babbling. She's not smoking, but she always comes with me to keep me company. You can say that we've been almost inseparable since that disastrous night with my father and the police last year.

When Claire started to act out soon after that, I thought it had to be connected with what she found out about my family situation and about the ongoing abuse. She was obsessed with keeping an eye on me, and turned downright possessive when someone approached me. Soon, she started to seriously freak out other kids at school, and the teachers also took notice of her erratic behavior. Claire's father was called by the school counselor, and they advised him to take his daughter to see a psychiatrist. Claire was diagnosed with a case of bipolar, just like her mother, and soon enough they started stuffing her with drugs to make her "normal".

I won't say that every day with my best friend is a blessing because when she's off, then it's fucking hard to witness and deal with, I won't lie. But we've been going through everything together so far. The good and the bad.

I stomp on the cigarette and turn to Claire.

"...and I thought that cloud looked like Johnny Depp, but Ms. Miller told me I shouldn't look at the sky during tests..."

I grin and cut in the middle of her tirade. "Hey, how about we skip our last class?"

That immediately gets my friend's attention, but she looks doubtful. "Oh, I don't know, Jenny. Since they've switched my medication, I'm not doing so well at school lately. It's all messy in there." She taps on her forehead. "Maybe I shouldn't skip classes for now."

"Are you sure? We can take a bus and go to the Mall or something. We could wander around shops and role-play being the hooker from Pretty Woman. And we could even go to that place that serves your favorite ice cream," I add in a singsong voice.

"Ooh, I love that. Damn Jenny, now I'll get stuck on all the fun I'm not getting while sitting in my history class. Staying will be pointless." She whines, but already straightens from the wall and lifts her backpack from the ground.

A grin stretches on my face. "You don't say. I totally didn't know that would happen."

"Bitch," Claire mutters, but already locks our arms together as we head out.

We're walking side by side through the school parking lot when I feel someone's eyes on me. Despite my better judgment, I turn my head to the side and am met with no one other than my latest pain in the ass.

Marcus and his group sit in the grass, enjoying their break under the large tree right by the path to the school's sports field. Most of them are chatting and not paying us any attention.

Claire and I, sort of, went our separate way last year and stopped going to the Mill and hanging around those douchebags. It might have something to do with overhearing

26

them making jokes out of Claire's illness and me telling them to eat shit. But also, I was just tired of the whole scene anyway.

Now, I curse under my breath when Marcus stands up, his spiteful glare focused fully on me.

Let's just say, he didn't deal with our "breakup" very well. And as it turns out, rejection can be a pretty strong motivator for hating someone, so now I can already predict what comes out of that jerk's mouth even before he speaks.

"Look who it is! Queen ice-cold bitch and her loony sidekick!" Marcus calls, drawing not only the attention of his friends but also of the people heading toward school before the bell rings out.

Claire claps in fake excitement next to me. "Have you heard it? I'm a queen's sidekick. Cool!" I smirk at my friend and decide to ignore the screaming idiot as we continue walking.

"Skipping school? What will daddy do when he finds out? It's supposed to be hot out next week, it's gotta be shitty covering it all up with clothes," Marcus taunts with an evil laugh.

I stop abruptly and detangle my arm from Claire's to turn around and walk a few steps back, my posture rigid.

"What the fuck is that supposed to mean?" I seethe, through clenched teeth.

"Oh, baby, don't get me wrong. I know you can be wild in bed, but you ain't exactly the BDSM type, so I know all those bruises you are always so desperately trying to hide aren't from you slutting it up," the fucker replies loudly for all to hear with a sick grin.

Red-hot fury envelops me on the spot covering my shame, and I charge toward him with clenched fists. The rest of the group stands up, and a girl named Ella shoves his arm. "Not cool, Marcus. Leave her alone."

"This doesn't concern you, Diaz, I don't need you defending me." I throw her way before refocusing on my target.

The bell rings in the distance, announcing the end of the break, and out of the corner of my eye, I see everyone gathering their stuff and heading to class, leaving only me, Marcus and Claire in the school lot.

I step closer to get right in Marcus's face threateningly. "You don't know what the fuck you're talking about. But if you won't stop spreading rumors, I will make you. Don't think I won't use everything I have to bring you down with me. Remember, I am not the only one with dirty laundry here."

He snorts. "Oh yeah? I think you don't know shit."

"I know what you are doing to get the extra money. So, if you cross me again, the sheriff will know too." It's my turn to laugh evilly as I see Marcus's face paling. "Think you're so fucking clever, huh? I know exactly where you get your party favors from."

A loud whistle rings around, and we all turn to look in the direction of the noise. A black shiny car is parked on the other side of the road, and behind the wheel sits no one else than the object of my desires, also known as Officer Brody.

"Oh look, here is my friend that works for the police. Maybe he'll be interested in our conversation about selling illegal substances. Shall we ask him?" I ask with feigned casualness, backing a step toward the parking lot.

Marcus grabs my arm harshly and draws me closer before he whispers in my ear. "Maybe I should thank you for showing me what a piece of trash you are. I feel sorry for the next fool who falls for your skanky ass."

I'm shoved away roughly and almost lose my footing before the sound of an opening car reaches my ear. Regaining my balance, I wave that I'm fine before the fucking Hulk comes to my rescue, bulldozing everyone in his way. I don't want any more unnecessary drama, so when Brody doesn't immediately go back to the car, I gesture for him to cut it out forcefully and shake my head. After a moment of hesitation, he backs off and proceeds to wait in a car with an unhappy expression on his face.

"So that's who you've been fucking?" Marcus, who's been watching our silent exchange, sneers, drawing my attention back to him.

I sigh and cross my arms. "No, it's not. But it isn't your business whom I'm sleeping with, it never was."

I turn to Claire, who's been watching the whole scene unbothered.

"Let's see what Brody wants."

Claire's face lights up immediately, and she starts bouncing toward the dark car, with me trailing after her.

"Ooh, nice car, Officer. Black is your color. Did you come here to give us a ride? Do you like ice cream by any chance?" Claire attacks the poor guy right away. She loves making him uncomfortable with her cheery friendliness.

He scratches his head. "Uh, I guess? Hey, Claire, do you mind if I speak to Jen for a minute?"

"Sure. But don't be too long, you two. Jenny has promised me some whorish role play and ice cream afterward." Claire chirps with a sincere expression before turning around and walking away to sit on a bench nearby.

Brody's eyebrows lift above his sunglasses. "Do I even want to know what the fuck it means?"

"You wouldn't understand. It's a girls' thing," I reply and smooth down my hair.

"How come?" Brody asks, the one corner of his lips turning up.

"How come you're not a girl? Well, for one thing, I assume you have a dick."

He groans and shakes his head. "Why did I even ask?" Then he peers at me from under his sunglasses and motions to the passenger seat with his head. "Get in."

I roll my eyes and stay put.

We started this weird thing between us two weeks after Claire called the police. Brody sought me out at the town's fair and basically informed me he knew what was happening at my house and tried to convince me to report my father to the police. After I told him to get lost, he got more determined to help me and started following me around and checking up on me every chance he got. I don't exactly understand why he's so bothered by my situation, but I allow him to watch over me, for selfish reasons mostly – him looking so damn good being the main one. It's also nice to have someone other than Claire give a shit.

Sadly, Brody doesn't seem to reciprocate my feelings and usually treats me like the petulant teenager that I probably am to him. He's older, and I'm underage, so I get it, but a girl can always dream. You don't exactly choose your first-ever crush. But the fact that he's not interested in me like that doesn't mean I can't have some fun while teasing him. I love making him uncomfortable with my sexually overcharged comments. And I am proud to say that I even made him blush once or twice. I regret not recording it with my phone, it was hilarious.

I guess you could say that we are sort-of-friends now.

"Boyfriend of yours?" Brody asks, nodding toward Marcus, who's probably still glaring at me from across the road, and removes his glasses, giving me a clear view of his intense eyes.

Instead of going around and getting in Brody's car, I lean into the open window, rest my elbows on the frame and push my boobs right in his face in the process.

"What's it to you? Are you jealous?" I tease.

Not surprisingly, he's not at all impressed with me, but involuntarily glances down before snapping his eyes back at me. "No," he deadpans. "But I didn't like the view of him manhandling you."

"Oh, you're worried about me. That's so sweet," I coo with a smile.

When he doesn't answer and just continues to glare at me, I sigh and move back from the window.

"Not a boyfriend. His name is Marcus. Just someone I used to fuck, if you must know."

Brody scoffs. "Thought you would have better taste in men, considering."

"Officer, are you proposing something?" I waggle my eyebrows.

"Stop with this shit," Brody responds, his voice dark. "That's not why I'm here today."

"So, what brings you here? I doubt you came to stalk me on school grounds only to ask me about my sex life."

"I didn't..." He growls, but shakes his head and starts again. "First, technically we're not on school grounds here."

"Sounds exactly like something a predatory stalker would say," I mumble.

Brody ignores me and continues. "Second, I'm not stalking you, I'm just looking for you, so we could talk. I came all the way here to ask you about something privately, so can you please get in the car?" he asks, in a tone that indicates he's done with me trying to be funny.

I grimace, but begrudgingly get into the passenger seat. I can already guess what is it that he wants to ask me. It always goes similarly. He wants me to admit that I'm abused and file a report. I tell him to fuck off, and he will get angry and frustrated. I will get defensive and the next thing you know, the doors are slumming. Next week he will seek me out again and we will continue with this bullshit. Why bother? I wonder what's in it for him if I fuck up my father's reputation by running my mouth.

After I'm seated, I look between the two of us and chuckle. "You know, this looks shady as fuck that you are luring underage girls into your car right outside of school."

"If someone had a problem with it, I would just tell them that you're my informant," he states calmly in a husky voice.

I look at him incredulously. "What the fuck, Brody? So, not only will I be seen as a trashy slut, but you also want people at school to think that I'm a fucking narc?"

He frowns at me. "Why would anyone call you a slut?"

When I just snort disdainfully, he sighs and drops the subject, only to switch to his law enforcement routine.

"Did you think more about my proposition?"

I pick at my nails and ask, "What proposition would that be?"

"Don't play with me, Jen. You know this is about your safety. How are things at your house?"

"The usual," I answer and look away.

Brody snorts. "That could mean anything in your case. But at this point, I would be surprised if you responded differently. There's something else I wanted to talk about."

I look back at him, and can tell he's not sure if it's the right call to share with me.

"I didn't think it was an issue before, but I've been keeping an ear out to try and maybe get something useful on the sheriff. For a while now, there's been rumors about your father drinking on the job and getting reckless or using too much force. For now, people are tight-lipped, just whispering, but I wonder if they're not covering for him with other things too."

I mask my reaction with a bored expression and slump in the seat. "I don't know what you want me to say. I have no idea why people think it's okay to spread rumors like that about their boss."

Brody hits the steering wheel in frustration, making me jump. "Damn it, Jen. I want you to tell me if he's been getting worse. I want you to tell me what the fuck is going on, so maybe I could help you. Not only that, but I want to bring this motherfucker down, so he doesn't hurt anyone ever again."

"Why the fuck do you care?" I ask, throwing my arms up in exasperation.

"I just do!" he booms.

"You're fucking obsessed or something. Ever since you came to fucking Bell Ridge, you're on a mission to be a pain in my ass. I told you, I don't know what the fuck you are on about. Everything is fucking fine! If you have problems with your boss, do something about it yourself, don't fucking use me in your vendetta against my father!"

Brody rears back, offended. "That's not what I'm doing, Jen. God-damn it!"

"Oh yeah? You always want me to be open with you, but you're never so open when it comes to your motives!"

"I'm a fucking police officer, that's what I'm supposed to be doing." He growls.

"Funny. Where's your uniform, Officer?" I ask mockingly. "Where's the police car, huh? Why are you questioning a minor without the parent's consent?"

When Brody starts to stare out of the windshield, breathing heavily and doesn't reply, I mutter, "That's what I thought."

I move to get out of the car, but before I can open it, Brody touches my arm and with a pleading expression says, "Jen, it's complicated, but I promise it's not what you're thinking. I'm not trying to use you, I want to help you. Truly."

After I shake off his hand, I get out without a response. I look for Claire and find her sitting right where I last saw her playing on her phone.

I take a few steps from Brody's car and stop when he calls after me.

"Jen, do you still have my number?"

Without looking in his direction, I call back, "Yeah."

"Will you call if you need my help?"

"No," I reply right away and then throw over my shoulder, "Till the next time, Handsome."

• • • •

AFTER CLAIRE AND I left the school grounds, we hopped on the bus and I spent the whole ride telling my friend what I learned from Brody. At first, she didn't comment, but as soon as she had her ice cream in hand, she was on my case.

"I think you should tell him everything, Jenny. Maybe he can help. I wish I could be the one to do something about your dad, but Lord knows I'm fucking useless," she says with a disgusted face.

I take her free hand in mine and force her to look me in the eyes. "Claire, you're not useless. You're brilliant. You wanted to help me many times, but I told you no. It's my choice. I love you even more for not taking that choice away from me."

Claire shakes her head, irritated, but doesn't say anything else as she attacks her ice cream cone.

I look at my half-melted one and sigh, not really in the mood to wander around the mall, now that we're here.

The reason Brody struck a chord today more than usual, is that my father had been drinking more and more lately, and the violence had been progressing. Mainly when it comes to my mother, as I barely get out of my room nowadays.

When I didn't stick my nose out, and managed to avoid his wrath for almost a month, he finally had to come to the conclusion that my vacation is long overdue. For the first time in years, he came knocking, and when I didn't open, he had broken down the lock.

He didn't hurt me too bad considering, but there was a new kind of darkness lurking in his eyes, and it scared me more than any physical violence ever could. The looks he throws my way now that I'm grown, seem almost sexual, yet I'm hoping it's just my wild imagination. He may be a psychopath, but I don't think he would ever cross that line. I try to convince myself of that each time I enter my lockless room because the alternative makes me queasy.

I break out of my depressing thoughts and throw away what's left of the ice cream into the dumpster before sitting back down next to Claire.

Then I nudge her with my shoulder. "Claire, relax. Everything will be okay. This is my life. I'm used to it."

She turns her head in my direction so fast, I am surprised she doesn't have a broken neck. "That is so fucking wrong, Jenny! You shouldn't be fine with it. No one should get used to it. It makes me furious how casual you always act about it. If something happens, I will lose you forever. I can't lose you! You are the only person that matters!" Claire snaps, her face twisting in anger.

"Hey, stop it." I try to soothe her with a gentle voice so she doesn't spiral in a public place. I know her moods, and this look on her face doesn't bode well for me. When she's down to a certain point, it's hard to calm her down.

I take both of her hands and put them on my face. "Can you feel me? I'm here. I'm not going anywhere, Claire. Promise, I will always be here."

She blinks at me for some time, her breathing calming as she comes back from whatever dark place her mind visits when she's scared.

"You can't promise me that," she mutters, her eyes getting that faraway look I hate again.

"Well, tough shit. Because I am." I slap my hands on my thighs and stand up. "Come on, we have to catch the bus."

"Yeah, I guess..." Claire grumbles with a sour face before we head out.

One week later, I'm walking the distance from Claire's to my house, after spending the entire afternoon watching stupid movies and eating junk food.

It had been a perfect last few days. Claire was in a good mood, and my father was barely present at the house. He's supposed to be working on some big case. Honestly, I don't give a shit where he's at as long as it's far away from me.

However, when I see that my father's car is already parked in the driveway, I feel my good spirits evaporate. I feel a sense of foreboding as I reach for the doorknob, but I quickly shake it off.

I enter and walk through the hallway to find my mother bustling about in the kitchen. I come to her and kiss her cheek before casting her a questioning look. We always walk around the sheriff on our tiptoes, but today's silence seems to be charged with something bad. I can't pinpoint what it is exactly.

Mom bends her neck to look through the doorway into the living room. Then she whispers, "Your father is in a weird mood today. He came in, didn't say a word, just sat down and poured himself a glass of whiskey. He's been sitting like that for an hour, casting suspicious looks my way every so often. I can't remember if I did something wrong in the morning." She rakes her hand nervously through her hair.

Okay, that is unusual for him to be quiet, but I suppose it's better than him wiping the floor with my mother's face or screaming insults at us.

I shrug and then whisper, "What about dinner?"

My mother bites her lip and then walks quietly toward the fridge and takes out a wrapped-up plate for me. "I thought it'll be better if you go eat in your room. I don't know what all of this means."

I nod my head in a thank you, and then slowly walk away from the kitchen before going to my room, closing the door silently behind me.

Maybe today will be one of the days without violence, I think to myself as I eat the cold dinner on my bed. I can only hope.

It's almost time to get to sleep when I hear a loud shriek and glass breaking somewhere in my house. I jump up from the bed and consider my next move. Normally, I would just turn off the lights and pretend that I'm not here, or jump out the window and go to see Claire. But after the talk with Brody last week and my father acting strangely today, something keeps me rooted in place.

I'm standing in the middle of my room, barely breathing, listening to the terrifying sounds.

When the fight gets closer to my bedroom, I can make out my father's words and the sounds of a fist punching a body. My mother's yelps resonate with each hit.

"Tell me the truth, you fucking whore! You've probably been spreading legs for everyone with a dick back at the base. I fucking knew it!"

"No, David, I swear. I don't know what you're talking about." She whines brokenly before another hit sounds through the house.

"You fucking bitch! I fucking hate you! You're pathetic!" I hear a loud thump and then my mother begging for him to stop.

"You're a disgusting whore! I had a feeling that little slut in there wasn't even mine!"

"No! David! I swear, I don't know what you're talking about!" My mom starts sobbing.

"You disgust me," he says coldly before something slams hard into my door, making me jump, my mother's cries dying down immediately.

I cover my mouth to hold my frightened squeak when I hear steps and see my door handle moving. I whirl around and run to the window, trying to escape, but my body is pushed to the wall before bouncing back right into my father's sweaty palms.

"Where do you think you're going?" he asks mockingly before throwing me on the bed. I try to get up, but he jumps on me, crashing my chest with his knee.

I struggle to get him off, but he's too heavy. He punches me hard in the side of the head and I immediately see stars. My body loses its fight for a second, and my father uses this moment to squeeze my neck.

I begin to choke as he spews in my face, the strong smell of whiskey in his breath making my eyes sting as I try to draw some air into my lungs. "You fucking slut! You're just like your mother. I never saw the resemblance, and now I know why. You're not even fucking mine!"

I'm on the verge of blacking out when he lets go of my throat and begins to unclasp his belt.

"I will fucking show you! Heard rumors about you giving it up to everyone. Now, after all these years, I can finally make some use of you." My father slurs and continues to unbutton

40

his jeans, and then proceeds to reach into my pajama bottoms. He shoves his fingers roughly right into my panties.

If the pain wasn't so severe, I would've sworn it wasn't real. It can't be happening. My father is about to rape me right in my bed.

I begin to struggle with renewed energy, hitting my father with an elbow to the head and making him howl in anger. He punches me in the side of the head again, making my skin split over my eye. I try to throw him off me again, but I feel powerless and weak as he pulls my shirt up and roughly grabs my breast, making me cry out in pain.

I can feel his arousal through his pants where he's pressed to me, and I almost vomit in my mouth as he licks the uninjured side of my face. Turning my head away in disgust, I catch the sight of the bedside lamp. Using to my advantage the fact that my father lowered his head to explore my body, I swiftly reach for the lamp, and without hesitation slam it into his head with all of my might.

For a moment, I don't move, worried I didn't hit him hard enough, and knowing he'll kill me now, but then his body turns limp on top of me with blood oozing out of the back of his head. Clumsily, I crawl from under him and land on the floor like a sack of potatoes.

I lift myself slowly, my whole body is trembling. I chance a peek at the unconscious form and when I see his back moving with small breaths, I realize I don't have much time before he wakes up. Holding up to the wall, I walk to the door and find my mother passed out on the floor in the hallway. I kneel next to her and slap her lightly on the cheek as I whisper, "Mom, please wake up. We have to go."

I almost start hyperventilating when she doesn't open her eyes right away, but then she stirs and blinks rapidly before focusing her bloodshot eyes on me.

"Jenny. What happened?"

I help her sit up. "Mom, we have to go! Dad said... H-he tried...to rape me. We need to run!" I cry and my mom frowns.

"Oh no, baby. Where is he?" She looks around as if afraid my father will jump on her from some corner.

"I hit him with a lamp," I admit and ignore her horrified gasp. "We don't have much time, he can wake up at any moment," I whisper urgently, trying to lift my mother from the floor.

She shakes her head and draws me toward her, something close to regret written on her face as she says urgently. "I'm so sorry, Jenny. Back when your father served in the military, we used to live at the base. There was this... Your father and I had a crisis, and Robert was a nice man... We had an affair," Mom whispers and looks away in shame.

"What? When was this?" I ask, completely shocked by my mother's confession. I crouch in front of her, forgetting about the impending danger.

"Before you were even born. I made a mistake and I regret it ever since. I tried to do everything in my power to make it up to David after that. He never suspected a thing. How did he find out? Why now? It's been eighteen years." Mom's eyes fill with fresh tears and her lower lip starts to wobble.

Putting away the shock of finding out my mother's secret, I ask, "Okay, what happened before he started screaming? What set him off?"

"I don't know, honey. He was sulking and drinking, but then he got a call. After he hung up, he threw the glass he was holding and started screaming that you're not his." She shakes her head in puzzlement.

"So, I'm not his?" I ask hesitantly, not knowing what I want the answer to be.

"Oh, no honey, don't worry. You are David's, I have no doubt." She takes my hand and turns even more serious. "But Jenny, you see how your father is. He will never believe me, now that he knows what happened back then. Or even if he only suspects."

"That's why we have to get the fuck away. He will kill us." I try to lift her by the hand again as I stand up.

I'm met with resistance and I look down at my mom in bewilderment. "Mom, we have to go. Help me out here."

She shakes her head and murmurs. "I'm not going anywhere."

"What?" My mouth drops in disbelief.

She nods to herself as if she already made up her mind, and then peers at me with a determined expression. "I love your father. He suffered a lot in life and I know we can come back to the way things were, Jenny."

I blink at her and retreat. "You're delusional. He won't change, Mom. He'll finally kill us."

"I made vows, Jennifer. For better and for worse. This is worse, but it will get better soon. I made some mistakes and he made some mistakes. I know we can make this all right. You just have to disappear for a while. Let him calm down and rethink everything. You're always triggering him, dear. He will calm down, and we will soon be back to the way things were."

I stare at my mother's crazed face, my eyes stinging from the unreleased tears. He's finally done it. He broke her. Or maybe she was always like this.

"It will be all right, Jenny. You'll be fine. You are strong like your father." She smiles softly, her eyes already dropping as she passes out. Beaten, amidst the broken glass, slouched by a blood-splashed wall.

I swallow down a scream and get into action, knowing that if I want to survive, I can't wait for my mother to get real. It's her choice. I'm making mine for the first time. If I don't, I will only be getting out of here in a coffin, and that isn't happening. Not today.

I switch on my survival mode and start thinking about strategy. Okay. I need clothes, money and somewhere to hide. Holding my breath as I reenter my room, and keeping an eye on my father's slumped form the whole time, I move to my closet to fish out my pre-prepared escape bag. I toss it out of the window and move to my father's lifeless body to take his keys out of his back pocket. Maneuvering my hand with a surgeon's precision, with the adrenalin spurring me on, I exhale in relief when my palm closes over the sharp metal. I snatch the keys and quickly retreat in the direction of my father's small office.

I've been here only a few times, as my mom and I were never allowed to get inside, but I know where my father keeps his stash. Just because he was throwing fists daily, doesn't mean I wasn't curious about what's so valuable in here. When I was younger and smaller, I spied on his ass constantly.

I open the door with the key and slip inside silently, walking straight to his desk. After I open the last drawer, I move the gun my father keeps in here away, and reach into the not-so-secret department. I take one wad of cash and leave the rest. There's gotta be at least fifty thousand stored in here, but I only take what I need.

I straighten from the desk and something on the side catches my eye. After pausing to make sure the house is still silent, I move to one of the folders at the top of the stacks.

It says *Brody, D.* on the top and I quickly open it to scan it briefly. Why was my father looking so closely into Brody?

Well, it doesn't matter because I don't think the sheriff found here what he's been looking for. There's nothing useful in here. But I do copy his address into my phone quickly before snapping the folder shut.

I see another one, this time the label says *Lepinsky, M.* and I frown. Why would the sheriff have Marcus's file at his house?

I'm just about to reach for it when I hear pained moaning from the other room, and I know my time is up. I leave the office and drop the keys by my mother's still sleeping form. Then I grab my shoes, which I left by the front door earlier, and sneak outside barefoot. Walking around the house, I slip the shoes on and go to collect my bag from under my window. I don't even look inside to see if my father has gotten up yet. I start running, and I never look back.

CHAPTER III

B^{rody}
I yawn as I get into my apartment after my shift at the station doing some shitty paperwork all day. I don't know how much longer I can do this. The sheriff was onto me from the start and is making my time here as insufferable as possible. I was supposed to get to Bell Ridge, investigate for six months tops, and move on to the next case, but it turned out to be more complicated than we originally thought. Add to that a certain smart mouth complicating things even further for me and here I am.

I walk straight to the fridge to grab a beer, massaging my stiff neck on the way. I untwist the cap and pull a large gulp, sighing in contentment at the feel of the cold, heavenly liquid. What a fucking day. No, scratch that. What a fucking week.

I eye my fridge one more time, considering heating up some food, but when I feel the tiredness weighing me down, I ignore my growling stomach and move to the living room to plop on the couch. I grab the TV remote and flip through the channels until I find some hero action movie and then put the volume on low. Staring at the screen, and not really seeing it, I am almost nodding off when my phone starts ringing. It's my private number, the one I only share with my friends and family. I take it out of my pocket and frown sleepily at the unknown caller before answering. "Hello?"

"Hey, Handsome. Did I wake you?" I hear a very familiar voice ask in a faked cheerful voice, sounding a little winded.

"Jen? Why are you calling? What happened?" I sit up in alert, sleep immediately forgotten. Jenny has never in almost two years called me so I know something must be seriously wrong.

Jenny sniffs and then answers casually, "Oh, you know, the usual teenage stuff." She clears her throat when I don't say anything, waiting for her to elaborate. "So, uh, Brody. You remember all of that about me needing help and then you showing up on your white horse to rescue me?"

I grunt in response, my body tense.

"You could say that now is the time," she admits reluctantly.

I stand up, ready to get on the road. "Where are you?"

Jenny sniffles again, and then instructs, "Turn around and look out the window."

"What?" I mutter, but automatically whirl straight to my window, only to rear back in surprise when I see the contour of someone's head in the darkness barely reaching the windowsill.

"How the fuck did you get up there?" I ask in bewilderment.

Her white teeth flash in the darkness as she grins at me through the glass.

"Unimportant. Focus. I need you to pull me in through the window," Jenny answers on the phone.

"Why didn't you just knock on the door like a normal person if you knew my address?" I argue, but start unlocking the window after putting the phone away. I lean out and see Jen balancing on the narrow metal step in between levels.

"What the fuck, Jen?! Did you jump here from the fire escape staircase?"

"Brody, I would love to chat about how fucking agile I can be, but I don't know how much longer I can hang onto the wall." She scolds me and I grab her outreached arm to pull her up. Jenny weighs next to nothing so I lift her easily, but on her way over she loses balance and tumbles fully into my arms. She starts to remove herself ungracefully, and I detect something off about her movements.

"Jen?" I watch her apprehensively as she sways a little.

She groans in pain, her wild hair obscuring the full view of her, and I move the dark curtain of locks away, only to pull away in shock when I get a full view of her busted face.

"Fuck," I mutter just as she starts to collapse. I lift her in my arms and rush to lay her down. She moans when her body meets the surface of the couch.

"My hero," she whispers jokingly before closing her eyes with a sigh.

"Shit, Jen. You need to go to the hospital." I start to straighten up to get my phone but am stopped by Jenny's hand snatching me by the shirt with surprising strength.

She opens one of her eyes and slurs tiredly. "No hospital, you promised I could trust you." Seeing the indecision on my face, she spits through clenched teeth, "No. Hospital. Or I'm fucking out of here."

"Good luck with that. You're barely fucking moving," I growl, agitated.

"Watch me," Jen replies before sitting up surprisingly fast and trying to get to her feet, almost falling from the couch in the process.

"Jesus Christ," I mutter and help her move to her previous position. "Fine. Be that way. I won't take you to a hospital. But you have to tell me what hurts."

Jen lies back on the couch and exhales heavily. "How about everything?"

I scan her body, only now noticing that she is wearing pajamas and dirty tennis shoes. Her arms and wrists are covered in red marks. The shirt she has on is torn in one place and dirty from the blood that was dripping from her face.

After asking for permission, I lift the hem of her shirt slightly and hiss at the state of her belly as I move my eyes to her midriff. It looks terrible, the skin black and blue.

"Fuck, sweetheart. You could have internal bleeding."

"I'll be fine. I just need to sleep a little." She waves me off and focuses on the ceiling as I sit on the coffee table in front of her.

"What were you thinking, jumping on buildings in your state? You could've seriously hurt yourself," I scold, but there's no real heat behind my words.

"I was thinking that there's a camera at the front entrance to your building, and I didn't want anyone to know that I'm here." Her expression is unimpressed, as if she thinks I'm a dumbass for even asking.

"Jen, we're on the third floor. How did you even know which window was mine?"

"I calculated my chances, and it turned out my calculations were correct. Get over it." She smiles, which makes me focus on her skin wrinkling around the dried blood and on the swelling on the right side of her face.

With a grunt, I get up and mutter, "I'll bring you some ice."

When I get back with a bag of frozen vegetables, I find Jenny still staring at the ceiling as tears drip silently from her face and into her tangled hair.

"Here, put this on your face, it will help. Do you want to wash up?"

Jen shakes her head but takes the frozen bag and lets out a hiss as it makes contact with her tender skin. Her eyes close as she exhales deeply, relaxing a little more on the couch.

"Sweetheart, what happened today?" I have to ask.

She doesn't answer me for so long, I think she'd fallen asleep, but then she mumbles. "We'll talk tomorrow, okay, Brody? For now, I need you to keep watch." Her eyes snap open, looking right at me. "Promise me, you won't stab me in the back and call anyone."

I'm not happy, but for the moment I would probably do anything she asked me for. "I promise, Jen. I won't. You can trust me. You're always safe with me."

"Thanks, Damon." Jenny sighs softly, using my first name for the first time since we met. She closes her eyes and falls asleep within minutes. The exhaustion visible on her bloodied face.

I take a blanket from the end of the couch and cover Jen's fragile form.

How could someone do this to their own child? Scratch that. How could someone do that to anyone?

Today's events only confirm what I knew all along. David Wallace has to be stopped and punished at all costs.

I slip into my bedroom and start pacing. My heavy breaths are the only thing I can concentrate on as I try to calm myself. If

51

I don't, tomorrow all they will be talking about in the news will be the sheriff's remains splattered all over fucking Bell Ridge.

Damn it all to hell. I failed her. I made a promise to protect Jen and to get her out. After I tried so hard to get this fucking bastard before something like this happened, I still failed. The investigation progressed too slow. And now, almost two years later, Sheriff Wallace is still running his little underground empire. He's still unreachable, and free to do what he wants. Free to hurt someone that I care about.

We are aware that he is involved in gun and drug trafficking. But proving that turned out to be a challenge. Or maybe I'm just shitty at it.

I never thought I would get so personally invested in this case, but when I saw Jen on the first night, something struck me. I couldn't take her haunted eyes out of my mind. She looked small and breakable, but what disarmed me on the spot was the hate and fire in her eyes. Jenny wasn't broken yet, she was a fighter. And I thought I need to do everything in my power to bring that monster down before her fire gets put out.

Despite my better judgment, I sought her out and tried to convince her to turn on her father and report him. At first, my supervisors were on board with the idea of bringing her on our side as an asset, after all, she could be a great source. But when there hasn't been a breakthrough with the stubborn creature, my boss told me directly to stop engaging with her and to try to find another angle. So, there went my plan to pull her out through legal channels as an informant.

But I didn't stop there. It was the first time in my career as an FBI agent that I went against direct orders and continued to meet with Jennifer whenever I could. At first, I saw her just as a teenager who needs my help. But then time went by, and she grew on me in a whole other way. After some time, it was harder and harder to look at her beauty, hear her smart ass comments and deal with her shameless flirting.

It's getting difficult for me to ignore the attraction I'm feeling toward her, but I'll do everything in my power to distance myself from it. I turned thirty-one this year, and I feel like a fucking creeper even thinking about Jen in that way. But I guess attraction doesn't always follow logic or propriety. Needless to say, though, I would never cross that line with her. This isn't why I'm helping her at all.

When I squash the murderous thoughts and feel more composed, I go to my bathroom to grab the first aid kit before going back to Jenny. She hasn't moved since I left, but her breathing turns erratic when I kneel by her and reach toward her face with a wet towel to clean the blood.

I barely touch her skin when she starts thrashing around.

"No! Get off me!" Jen whimpers with a broken cry in her sleep.

Startled, I drop the towel and then quickly take her hand and put it on my chest, right above my wildly beating heart. I move closer, careful not to touch her anywhere, and whisper in her ear soothingly. "Shh, it's only me, sweetheart. You're safe. Everything is all right. I will protect you. Jen, I promise."

I repeat my words a few times before the girl hiccups in her sleep and relaxes. I pick up the towel again to clean her, happy when there's no resistance this time. There isn't much I can do to help when she's asleep. So, after cleaning the blood as well as I can, I put some ointment on the cut on her eyebrow and then change the warming pack to a fresh one. It will have to be enough for now.

I bring an armchair next to the couch, turn off the light and get comfortable there before closing my eyes. I could go to my bedroom and leave the door open, but I'll feel better staying closer in case Jen needs something.

As I'm falling asleep, I still wonder if I'm doing the right thing. Maybe I should be firmer about taking Jen to see a doctor, or maybe I should've reported the whole incident to my boss. Fuck, my head is a mess. This entire case is a mess.

But I guess it's too late to back out now.

• • • •

I FEEL HER STARE EVEN before I open my eyes.

"Take a picture, it will last longer," I grumble, my voice still heavy with sleep.

"How'd you know I didn't already?" Jen questions from somewhere close to my left.

I turn my head in that direction and smell fresh coffee wafting through the air. Opening one eye, I find Jen already dressed in jeans and a fresh shirt, her bare feet planted on the carpet as she's holding up a steaming mug. One side of her face looks like someone has mistaken her for a punching bag, but otherwise, she looks like on any other day. Not a hair out of place. The bruises on her body fully covered by her clothes.

I blink my other eye open before shifting in my seat and groaning when I feel how stiff my muscles are. I get to my feet and stretch, my joints popping loudly with the strain.

"Is this what the elderly life looks like?" Jen asks in a playful voice, as she's sipping from her mug, looking me up and down shamelessly.

"Watch it," I warn her with a stern look and then check the time, frowning when I see it's after nine already. How did I sleep through her busting about in my apartment?

Jen makes an innocent face. "I was gonna say, the elderly looks mighty fine on you."

I ignore her and move to the kitchen to pour myself some coffee. The annoying creature comes after me and jumps up effortlessly to sit on the counter, her legs swinging back and forth. After I take a sip and feel more like a human again, I decide it's time for the little lady to provide me with some answers. I turn to her fully and lean on the counter.

"Okay, Jen. The jig is up. Tell me what happened."

She moves her mug to the side and then crosses her arms stubbornly.

"Please, don't be difficult. Not after what I saw yesterday. Your father did this?" I gesture toward her face.

At the word "father", she flinches slightly, but otherwise keeps her expression neutral as she answers with a simple "Yes."

"All right. No surprise. And how often does something like this happen?"

She shrugs and averts her gaze. "I don't know... Sometimes?"

"Why didn't you go to the police or report your father when I asked you?"

Jen casts me a quick patronizing look. "Not exactly in the position to trust the police."

"But you trusted me enough to come here," I state.

She shakes her head and looks away. "Didn't have anywhere else to go, and you offered your help many times."

"Fair enough. Okay. Is your mother aware of the abuse?"

Jenny snorts and answers bitterly, getting a little worked up. "Of course, she's fucking aware, she's had it fucking worse."

Shit. I probably should be more delicate about the whole thing, but it's hard not to punch my fist through the wall when I hear about women getting hurt by the hand of a man who's supposed to protect them. "Then where is she now?" I ask in a slightly gentler tone.

Tears spring into Jenny's eyes, but she keeps them at bay. "Mom told me to leave. Wanted to stay with him even after everything. Says she loves him."

"Not unusual in cases with spousal abuse," I grunt.

"We're not a fucking case! She's my mother, we're all just people!" She fumes, her arms uncrossing to grab onto the edge of the counter.

I nod and decide to change the subject. "What exactly happened yesterday?"

She mulls over her answer and then sighs. "Look, Brody. Thank you for letting me crash here, you are a godsend, truly. But this is still private. As soon as I have a plan in motion, I'm out of here. So, we don't need to do this. I'll disappear, and you will be free of whatever it is that makes you care about my situation."

"God damn it, Jen! Not this shit again." I slam my coffee mug on the counter and march closer to Jenny, who looks startled. Her eyes widen as she looks up at me.

I feel like an asshole for yelling, but I can't contain my frustration when she's being so... so fucking Jen.

"You have no idea how dangerous your father truly is! I can't tell you the details, but trust me, beating on women and children is not his only sin. I need to know everything, so I can help you create said plan so we can potentially do something about it. You're a fucking minor, Jen! If you still refuse to press charges and continue to lie for him, then there's nothing that I can do to stop him from coming after his runaway daughter! How do you think this will end? The first police patrol that catches sight of you will be on your ass and soon enough you'll be back at your house with him!"

Jenny's face turns white, her eyes dashing to the side. She grabs her throat and gulps loudly.

Shit. Way to go, man.

I try to think of a way to console her but curse when my phone starts ringing. Seeing it's from work, and I can't ignore it, I tell Jen I have to take this. She gives me a nod, and I walk out to get the call in my bedroom.

"Brody," I mutter impatiently.

"Hey, man. It's Diaz."

The chirpy voice of the police officer grates on my nerves, but I swallow my annoyance down and respond with, "Oh, hey. What's up?"

"It's all good. Hey, listen. I'm sorry to be calling you on your day off, but I know the guys don't always keep you in the loop so I just wanted you to know that something big happened with the sheriff yesterday."

I straighten up and hold the receiver tighter in my hand, now fully engaged in the conversation. "What kind of something are we talking about?"

Diaz clears his throat and I can hear him moving before there's a sound of doors closing. Then he says in a hushed voice, "Look, I observe stuff, and I know you hold a special interest in our shady boss."

"I don't know what you're getting at," I mumble and sit on my bed.

"Yeah, yeah. I know. The thing is, I'm not a fan of the sheriff either, and my kid goes to school with his daughter. I heard some rumors. If they're true or not, I'm not certain. What I do know is that some things here ain't right."

I'm gesturing with my hand as if he could see me. "Diaz, get to the point."

"All right. Yesterday, after you left, we got a call from the sheriff himself to send a patrol and an ambulance to his house."

"Who was the ambulance for?" I inquire, already assuming it was probably for Jen's mother. Poor woman.

"That's the thing, it was for the sheriff himself," Diaz says excitedly, surprising me.

When I don't reply right away, Diaz continues with his story and I can tell that it brings him immense joy to be, for once, the one with hot gossip.

"The thing that's fucking suspicious as all fuck is that he claims his daughter has assaulted him and her mother, stole some money, and then ran away from home."

"No way would anyone believe that she's capable of that," I snort.

"And here's where you're wrong. The girl's mother has backed his story up. So now that Jennifer girl is wanted for questioning."

"Motherfucker," I growl as I rub my forehead.

58

"Exactly my thoughts. I didn't get on the scene, but I heard it was a mess. The place was trashed. They claim she was drugged and enraged with her parents trying to discipline her." It's my colleague's turn to snort at his own words before he continues. "I know the girl has some issues, but it's hard to believe she could cause all the damage on her own. I mean, we're talking about overpowering an ex-military man and her mother at the same time."

"Yeah..." I grouse and stand up. "Thanks for the call, man. I appreciate the info."

"Don't know what you're talking about, brother. We're just two police officers talking about police stuff. Anyway, gotta go. Take care, man."

"Thanks, Diaz. You too," I mutter and end the call.

"Fuck." I tug on my hair in frustration before leaving my bedroom. I find Jen sitting on the coffee table, her head tilted in question.

"What's up with you and sitting on the furniture," I complain before going back to the kitchen.

She gets up to trail after me. "Was the call about me?"

I pretend not to hear her and bend to open the fridge before asking in a casual voice, "Bacon and eggs fine?"

Jen scoffs and nudges my thigh with her foot after sitting on the counter again. I glance up at her. "Don't say you're fucking vegan or something."

I have to hide my smile when she rolls her eyes dramatically. "Bacon and eggs are fine. But you didn't answer my question."

"What question was that?"

"Oh my God, you're annoying!" she whines, making me smirk.

"So you admit it's annoying when someone doesn't answer your direct question?" I ask evenly.

"You're insufferable," she informs me.

"And you're a brat," I clip back with no heat.

"Whatever, old man." She sticks out her tongue at me and jumps down from the counter, taking a seat at the table to wait for breakfast.

I shake my head and get busy preparing the food. I get us both a plate before sitting down across from Jen and digging into my eggs. After a moment of hesitation, she picks up her fork and starts eating too, casting glances at me here and there, but I ignore her completely and enjoy the momentary silence until I can.

When we're both finished, I clean everything up and then walk into the living room, ordering Jen to follow me with a jerk of my head. I sit down on the couch, resting my elbows on my thighs, and Jenny takes a seat opposite me in the armchair, her face tense.

"Earlier, that was a call from the station. Your father is not playing around. He claims that you have attacked him and your mother, and then stole some money before splitting. The police are currently looking for you to bring you in for questioning."

"What?!" Jen gapes at me in disbelief.

"Yeah. It doesn't look great. So, I think you have two options. The first option is going to a hospital, getting your injuries on the official record, and filing a counterclaim against your father."

"But then it's my word against his, right?"

I shift uncomfortably. "More than that, it's your word against both of your parents. Your mother supports his version for now."

"Of course she does. I'm not even surprised at this point. So, what's the other option?"

"You hide and wait it out," I offer reluctantly.

"Okay. Option b it is then." Jen slaps her thighs with her palms and moves to stand up but I stop her with my hand.

"Wait. It's not that simple. We have to think it through. For now, you're safe here and no one knows you're still in town. So, we have a day or maybe two to come up with something. You can sleep on the couch, I don't mind. But you're a minor that will need to get back to school at some point, I don't want you to miss out too much. I have some trusted people I can reach out to, and maybe they will be able to offer you a place. We can work on getting you emancipated from your parents. But I need some time to figure out how to make them drop the charges first."

"I'll be eighteen in a couple of months. And I don't give a fuck about school. I probably wouldn't even graduate at this point. Can't I just lie low until I'm an adult? Earlier, you said my father did some bad stuff, I'm assuming it's something illegal. Can't we just blackmail him to drop the charges, and I would go on my merry way?"

"Leave your father to me. I'm sorry, but I can't tell you more than that. There's a certain way to do things. Meanwhile, I want you to be safe and finish school, that's what we'll be focusing on."

Jen snorts and stands up abruptly. "Okay. What about Claire?"

"What about her?" I ask, annoyed with the sudden change of subject.

"Can I call her from your phone, to tell her what's going on? I can't find my cell. If the word got out, she'll hear about everything at school. She'll be sick with worry."

"I took your cell. Safer that way," I inform her and watch as her lip curls up in disdain before I pass her my phone.

"You can make one phone call. Tell her the most important things, but don't share any details. Don't tell her where you are. You don't know who's listening, and everybody knows you two are close. She'll be the first one to get questioned about your whereabouts. Knowing too much could put her in danger."

She nods absentmindedly, already clicking on the phone before locking herself in my bedroom. I scratch my chin as I stare at the closed door. I have to help her, I can't back out now, but damn is she testing my patience.

CHAPTER IV

Jenny

"Claire, it's me," I whisper as soon as my best friend picks up.

"Jenny? Oh my God, Jenny! When you didn't come to school, I didn't think much of it, assuming your dad got angry again and you couldn't show your face. But then I heard people whispering about something, and they were giving me strange looks. Stranger than usual. I eavesdropped on girls in the bathroom talking about you, and the stuff they were saying was crazy. Crazier than usual. Then after the first period, the police came to question me! It was just like in the movies, Jenny! It was scary, but also super exciting. Where are you?"

"Claire, breathe, babe. I can't tell you where I am." I sit down on Brody's bed and massage my aching head. "It's all so messed up. My father..." My voice breaks and I quickly wipe the unwanted tear escaping my eye.

"It's bad, isn't it? Are you okay?" she asks, her voice heavy with concern.

"It was bad, I got really hurt this time," I admit. "Claire, I... I'll have to disappear for a while. Things got so dangerous and... complicated, I can't tell you over the phone, and I don't know when it will be safe for me to come and see you or even call you again."

"Oh."

"I'm not leaving permanently. It's only temporary until everything settles," I rush to reassure her.

She sniffles on the other end of the receiver and answers in a heartbroken voice. "I knew this day would come. You were never safe, Jenny. I'm sorry I couldn't help you. Should have been more assertive and talked to my dad about taking you in. I should've done something."

"Nothing that happened is your fault, do you hear me? My father is a piece of shit, and it's all on him. He's the one making me run away. Not you, never you."

Claire continues as if I haven't spoken. "I did this. I hate myself so much, Jenny. If I wasn't so messed up, I would've helped you. Instead, I turned a blind eye, glad that you had only me to escape to, meaning you couldn't leave me. I felt needed. Don't you see it? My doctors, my father, even my stupid therapist, they are all right about us being toxic! But they are mistaken about me being the one who'll get hurt, it's you who was in danger all along. And now I will lose you forever!"

I hear my friend wailing uncontrollably, and my heart breaks for her. Hearing her pain through the phone breaks the dam on my own tears and I start crying too.

"Please, Claire. Don't think that. I love you and I need you so much. You're not losing me. I'll be back, I swear," I say even though I'm aware that it could possibly be a lie. I know there's a big chance I won't be back. But Claire will be okay, she'll be safer without me in her life. She's my soft spot, the one person my father can use against me, and I can't put her in jeopardy like that. Not my sweet friend.

I close my eyes and lie down on the bed, comforted by Brody's masculine smell surrounding me.

"Claire, are you still there?" I whisper when there's nothing on the other side for a while.

"Always," she whispers back.

"I need to know that whatever happens, you'll be all right. I need to know I still have you somewhere in the world. Safe and sound. Can you promise me that? No matter what?"

"Of course, Jenny. The same goes for you."

"I love you, Claire. I have to go. I don't know when I'll be able to contact you again."

"I understand," she says softly. "The important thing is that you're away from that monster. I'll be waiting. I love you too."

I close my eyes and grimace. "Bye."

"Goodbye."

I disconnect the call and stare at the white ceiling for a moment before taking a deep breath and sitting up. I groan silently, my whole body protesting at the sudden movement. Pretending like I could move normally in front of Brody took a lot of effort. I know he already saw me yesterday, bloodied and barely standing, but my pride can only take so much at this moment. So even though I would gladly stay on the comfy bed and take a much-needed nap, I lift my ass and walk out of the room searching for my grumpy rescuer. There's shit we need to go through before I can rest.

The living room is empty, so when I hear a murmur coming from the kitchen, I turn in that direction, slowing my movements once I make out Brody's voice talking to someone on the phone.

"...no, no. Of course, that wouldn't be wise. Yes, I understand your point, man."

I take a step closer and peek through the doorway. Brody's back is to me as he nods to whatever he hears on the other end.

"No. But I would rather not turn the girl in. There has to be another way... No, I won't fuck up the investigation, but by doing it your way, I would put myself in the spotlight too."

He tugs on his hair as if frustrated and growls. "Look, I get your point, and I know I've messed up, but I won't back out now, so you can either help me out or shut the fuck up and let me do the work. I've been here for two years, and we're almost there, I can feel it. But we have to deal with the girl first so she's not hurt even more in the crossfire."

Again, more listening, more nodding. "No, yeah, all right. No worries, I will get that motherfucker. He's getting careless, it's hard to cover your tracks when you're all over the place... Yeah, I will brief him when it's time. Don't make the call for now... Yeah, I'll call you when I know something. Yeah, later."

Brody ends the phone and hangs his head with a long sigh, then startles me. "It's rude to eavesdrop, Jen."

I walk into the kitchen and cross my arms. "How long did you know that I was listening?"

He turns his head to look at me and smirks. "Ever since you came in. I saw you lurking in the reflection of the microwave."

"Shit," I mumble as I glare at the damned treacherous device, and startle again when Brody starts laughing at me, his voice deep and rich. God-damn it, even his laugh is attractive.

I scowl at him to hide my real reaction to seeing his beautiful smile. "Good to see you're enjoying yourself." I snap my fingers. "Now, if you're finished with your comedic act, I think we still have some things to discuss. Who was that on the phone just now? And don't tell me it's not my business or ignore me again because I will seriously lose my shit," I end with a huff.

Brody's laugh dies down, but he still grins at me, his eyes crinkling at the corners. God, have mercy on me.

"We wouldn't want you to lose your shit. So, I guess we better get to it." He indicates for me to sit in one of the kitchen chairs.

"Gladly," I grouse, plopping down ostentatiously.

He shakes his head, but then gets serious again as he takes the opposite seat.

"Okay. I made a few calls and, unfortunately, staying here with me is out of the question for now. The good news is, I found you a place at the women's shelter in Madison."

When Brody sees the look on my face, he's quick to add, "Yeah, I know what you're thinking, but you'll be safe there. And remember that this is only meant to be a temporary solution, just to get you out of town until I can straighten everything out."

"What if you can't?"

He casts me a questioning look from across the table so I clarify. "What if you can't straighten it out? What if my father wins? What then?"

"I won't let that happen," Brody states with conviction, his face determined. "I promised you safety, and I intend to keep my promise."

When I give him a dubious look, he frowns and looks away as if considering something, then focuses back on my face, sitting up straighter in his chair.

"All right, I guess there are some things I could share with you so you're not in the dark completely."

"Go on."

"Okay... I'm a federal agent working undercover as an officer to infiltrate the local police. Your father is the main object of my investigation, but not exclusively."

When I lift my eyebrows while crossing my arms, he questions, "Really? No comment?"

Rolling my eyes, I respond, "There isn't much that can truly surprise me at this point, Handsome. Also, it makes total sense." I gesture for him to continue.

"Umm, okay. So, we are working on exposing your father's deeds, but until we smoke him out, I can't do much about the charges brought against you. But we are closer to getting him, as things are getting out of hand in his little scheme. Your father is on a slippery slope and tries to save himself by all means necessary. He even contacted some of his old friends from his time in the military, hoping to get them on his side. But in reality, he dug himself a little deeper in the process."

"Does one of those friends happen to be named Robert by any chance?" I ask, remembering the name from my mother's confession.

"I think so," Brody replies slowly, eyeing me suspiciously. "Jen, do you know something?"

"Nah, just curious about someone my mother mentioned once," I deflect, not wanting to get into that conversation. What happened yesterday is still a big no-no for me to talk about.

Brody looks skeptical but lets it go, thank God. "So, as I was saying. It's only a matter of time now before we make his little empire collapse, and you'll be free of your father for good."

"So what does he do? It has to be something big for the FBI to send their spy to a fucking nowhere-town like Bell Ridge."

"I can't share the details of the investigation," he deadpans.

"Oh, come on! Whom am I going to tell?"

Brody gives me a blank stare and keeps silent. Asshole.

"Pfft, fine. Be that way. When am I leaving to get to the shelter then?"

"I'll drive you today after it gets dark. Safer this way."

I stand up from the table. "Great. Now, if you don't mind, I'm going to take a nap."

"Be my guest," Brody states, his face expressionless as he watches my movements.

"And I'll be taking your bed. That fucking couch is preposterous," I warn him and decide to ignore the twitching corner of his lips as I march out.

Just when I reach the doorway, I clear my throat and, without turning fully, say, "Thank you for helping me, Brody."

"You're welcome, sweetheart," he grunts as I walk out.

• • • •

WE SPENT THE WHOLE way over to the shelter in Madison in silence. After I cried myself to sleep in Brody's bed, I drifted into unsettling dreams full of cold, angry eyes and grabby hands touching me. I woke with a silent cry to the sound of knocking on the bedroom door and a deep voice informing me that it was time to go.

I thought that sleep would be the remedy for my sore body and suffocating depression, but after I got up, the unpleasant feelings just amplified, making me cranky and agitated. When I sat in the passenger seat of Brody's car, I switched on the radio, turned toward the window, closed my eyes, and pretended to fall asleep because I would rather not take out my raging feelings on him.

Now, I'm dreading the next time when sleep will pull me under. I wish Claire were close so she could lie next to me and tell me about whatever's on her mind, calming me down in the process and keeping me on the ground. I want to hold her hand as I fall asleep and feel the closeness of someone who would never harm me.

Currently, I don't know what will happen to me, and that amplifies my anxiety with each minute. Brody claims that my father will be behind bars soon. I believe that he thinks he's telling me the truth, I can see the determination and hatred for my father in his eyes whenever we touch on the subject. But let's be real here. My father may be slipping, but he still holds a lot of power in our town, with his officers backing him up at each step. And he's not stupid. If he has a file on Brody and is looking into him, that means that he's not fooled and at least suspects he has a mole among his staff.

Sure, it would be great if my father disappeared, and I could go back home to my mother and Claire, return to school and start living like a normal person my age. Sounds great. But my life was never great, and I'm not so naïve to think that everything will work out in my favor just because I want to. Men like my father always win. They hold all the power. They can do whatever they want. And I am just collateral damage in the whole scheme of things. Unimportant. Disposable. Just something to use, play with and discard when it's broken beyond repair.

I'm pulled out of my thoughts when the car stops and Brody turns off the engine.

"We're here."

I straighten up from my hunched position and look out the windshield at a withered and gloomy-looking building on a rough-looking street, illuminated by the streetlight.

My expression must've shown my doubt because Brody says, "I know it doesn't look great, but you'll be safe here and one of the women is a relative of mine. She promised to keep an eye on you. I want you to stay here until we find another solution so you can go back home."

"Okay," I mumble.

"Hey," Brody puts his hand on my arm. "I know you probably don't believe me. And why should you? I should've dealt with your father a long time ago, instead, I let him throw me off the loop one too many times, and you got hurt."

"Not your fault, Handsome. Honestly, you've been on my case a lot about reporting him. I have to admit you are a persistent fucker because there were times when I seriously considered it." I smile at him sadly.

"Should've been even more persistent than," he grunts with a frown as he removes his hand from my shoulder and threads it through his hair in frustration. "Each week I told myself that on the next one, I will get that fucker, and you'll be free of him. Weeks turned into months, and then it's been two years of me chasing my tail. Your father was always one step ahead of me somehow."

"Yeah, he knows how to play the psycho game. He probably has many friends in higher places and plenty of people in his pocket. Don't be so hard on yourself, Brody. It's

71

hard to go against someone who's always playing dirty. Also, I meant to tell you before we part, he had a file on you on his desk, I saw it before I ran away. That's where I got your address from."

"What was in the file?"

"Not much. Things like date of birth, address, and annotation about your time in the Marines. Whatever he was looking for, he probably didn't find there, but it doesn't mean that he's not watching you or something."

Brody harrumphs with a frown and deliberates on what I've just told him for a minute, then asks, "Now that we are sharing, is there anything else you know about your father that could help me bring him down? It could be anything, Jen."

"There might be something. I don't know if it's related to your case, but you told me about this Robert guy before..." I start hesitantly.

"Yeah, Robert Barnett. What about him?"

"Well..." My mother's face comes into my mind as she tells me the story, and I change my mind. "You know what? It's not related. Forget I said anything."

"Are you sure?" Brody asks suspiciously.

"Just... unrelated family drama. It's nothing," I mutter evasively.

He hums in his throat, eyeing me some more, then shrugs.

I stare at the old building, as Brody seems to still mull over something. He drums his fingers on his thigh, and then reaches into his jacket. "Here." He takes a few hundred out of his wallet and extends it toward me.

"What's that for?"

"You'll need money. I doubt you have everything you need in that small bag of yours. This will allow you to get some necessities." He tries to hand me the money again, but I move back.

"Brody, that won't be necessary. I have money. A thief, remember?" I gesture toward myself with a thumb.

"Wait. So, you really robbed your father?" Brody asks in astonishment.

"Um. Of course. How was I supposed to run away without any cash? I had to think fast. Are you going to give me shit about that, Officer?" I ask irritably.

"Depends. How much did you steal?"

"Three thousand dollars," I state proudly and lift my chin, daring Brody to comment.

However, he surprises me when suddenly a bright smile stretches on his face. "That's my girl."

"What? You're not going to lecture me or something?"

He shakes his head and takes the keys out of the ignition after putting his money back in his pocket. "You were in a dangerous situation, and you were able to hightail out of there and got everything you needed before finding your way to safety. I'm not going to lecture you. I'm impressed, Jen."

I look away to hide my own smile, not wanting to show how much his praise pleases me. "Whatever."

"So, are you ready?"

"Sure, let's do this." I sigh and exit the car to follow Brody. He rings the doorbell and we both wait, looking around the dark street. It's almost midnight and there's not a soul in sight, yet I still can't shake the feeling of being watched. From the way

Brody surveys our surroundings, I can tell he can feel it too. Maybe we're both paranoid.

The sound of opening doors snaps me back to the present, and I pivot to see a short, plump woman in a stained apron wearing a warm smile.

She looks Brody up and down, her hands on her hips, and then clips playfully, "Damon, long time no see. I would've thought you were abducted by the aliens if it wasn't for your calls, assuring me you're still there. Now come, boy, and hug your aunt!"

Brody smiles fondly at the woman and bends to hug her before kissing her on the cheek. "Aunt Ruth, it's nice to see you too. How's Uncle Frank doing?"

Ruth gives a dismissive wave and chirps. "Annoying the hell out of me like usual, but I wouldn't have it any other way." Then she turns her focus on me and smiles even bigger than she did at her nephew. "Oh, my! You must be Jenny. Where are my manners, keeping my guests standing in the doorway? Come in, come in!"

We step after her into the well-lit hallway, and I am surprised by how charming and clean it looks. I guess it's true what they say about not judging a book by its cover.

"Are you two hungry? We have some leftovers from dinner, I'm sure I can call Amelia to heat them for you."

"Thanks, Aunt Ruth, but I'll have to get going soon. Jen?"

I shift my weight from foot to foot nervously. "Um. No, thank you, though. I'm exhausted, so if it's possible..."

"Oh! Of course, darling, you must be dead on your feet. I'll show you to your room," Ruth exclaims happily before addressing Brody. "You coming, boy, or are we saying goodbyes?"

Brody clears his throat. "Yeah, I need to go, but if I could just have a minute with Jen."

"Of course, dear. Take care and remember about your old aunt occasionally, would you? A visit once in a while would be nice," she scolds the grown man, but her smile is teasing.

"Yes, I apologize for not calling, but my work..."

"What it is that you are trying to say, boy? That your job is more important than your family?" She waves before his face, pretending she's trying to smack him. He chuckles lightly before hugging her. They whisper something for a minute, and then she leaves with a wink. I follow her movements with my eyes until she disappears around the corner.

"I want you to have that." Brody hands me a small mobile phone when I refocus on him. "It has my number installed in it. I will call you with updates if I have any. And if something happens, I want you to call me immediately, too."

I look at the phone and back at Brody's unusually open face before pocketing the device. "Thank you, big guy. You didn't have to do all of this. You didn't have to go out of your way to help me."

"I know, but I wanted to."

"Why, though? I've been nothing but a pain in the ass since you met me. You told me that many times."

He looks at me intently for a second and then, lowering his voice, says, "But you're my pain in the ass. And you got under my fucking skin, Jen."

75

Brody lifts his hand toward my face, almost touching it, and then at the last moment, changes his mind, and ends up tucking a lock of my hair behind my ear instead.

Our eyes meet, and my breathing accelerates when he glances down for a moment. I have to fight with myself not to lick my suddenly dry lips. We stare at one another, each of us in a state of weird suspension. The feel of his hand in my hair causes goosebumps to spread all over my body.

The intense moment passes when Brody shakes his head and pulls away, removing his hand as if I burned him.

With a fast, "Call if you need me," he's gone, the door closing loudly after him.

Okay, what was that? Did he...? No. I won't be reading too much into it. My head is all messed up right now. I'm probably daydreaming or something. Come on, Jenny, get a grip.

I breathe slowly through my mouth and then collect my bag from the floor before turning in the direction of the staircase. A surprised yelp leaves my mouth as I almost run into someone.

"Oh, I didn't know you were still here. I mean, of course, you can be here. It's your place, I guess. I was just... saying goodbye to Brody. We didn't..." I scratch anxiously behind my ear as I explain myself to Ruth, who's wearing a knowing smile. I don't understand why I feel as if I were caught in a compromising situation. Nothing happened.

Luckily for me, she doesn't comment on whatever she saw or heard and just leads me to one of the common rooms and then shows me where the bathroom is. Even though the place is clean and well-kept, you can see that they are struggling with money. Everything here shows signs of usage, the furniture is mismatched and outdated. Still, it feels homely somehow. We reach the bedroom, I get to choose from two of the free beds, with three more already occupied by other women, who are sleeping soundly. After whispering my gratitude to Ruth and wishing her goodnight, silently I enter the half-lit room and remove my shoes before putting my bag next to the pillow. I doubt that anyone would steal my stuff, but it's better to be safe than sorry. I take out the phone I got from Brody and see it doesn't have access to the internet, but what it does have is some music stored on it. When I see a few of my favorite bands there, I smile widely. How did he know? Or does he listen to the same stuff as me? Seriously, that man is still a mystery to me. That's probably why he's so alluring.

I fish out my headphones out of my bag and put them on. When the first beats of the familiar song reach my ears, my body instantly relaxes. I lie down fully clothed and fall asleep within minutes.

CHAPTER V

B rody

There's a knock on the door and one of the female officers, named Leslie, sticks her head into the room. "Hey, Brody! You've got someone asking for you at the front desk."

"Who is it?" I ask absentmindedly, without lifting my eyes from the stack of papers on my desk. Ever since the disaster with Jen and the sheriff, most police officers in Bell Ridge were assigned to find her. Those who aren't in Wallace's good graces, meaning those who aren't so willing to kiss his ass and to turn a blind eye to his missteps, like Diaz and I, were pulled aside to do everything else. My desk is folding under the weight of petty crime cases and unpaid tickets.

"The kid says his name is Marcus, but wouldn't give me his last name."

The image of a sneering punk shoving Jen in front of the school goes through my mind, and I snap my head up to look at the woman. My paperwork forgotten for the moment.

"Did he say what's this about?" I straighten in my chair and click my pen anxiously.

"Nah, said he'll only talk to you and that it's super important," Leslie replies in annoyance. "You want me to get rid of him?"

"No, bring him in. Thanks."

My colleague nods and retreats from the room. I don't even have time to pull myself together or rearrange the disaster on my desk before she brings Marcus. I ask her to close the door on the way out and gesture to the twitchy-looking kid to take a seat.

"Hi, I'm Officer Damon Brody. Officer Collins said you have something significant to talk about. I'm all ears then. What do you need?" I motion for him to start as I sit back in my chair.

Marcus looks at me askance with contempt, but from the way his leg is twitching, I can see that my perusal is making him nervous.

"Name's Marcus Lepinsky. But I guess you know that from Jenny or whatever." He looks away and licks his lips. "Don't know what's the deal with you two, really, but I think..."

When I only lift my eyebrows and don't say anything, the teenager shakes his head and curses under his breath. I can see he's battling with himself whether to tell me what he knows, and years of interrogations have taught me to let guys like Marcus work it out on their own. So, I wait patiently until he exhales heavily and sits up from his slightly slumped position to look straight at me.

"Jenny and I used to be a... thing. I care for her. Probably more than she ever cared for me... Still do, even though she broke my fucking heart. She's a piece of work..."

Involuntarily, my hands clench into fists, but I keep my cool despite the fact I want to smack him already.

"I know what happens at her house. I know about the sheriff. And I know you know too."

"Know what?" I play ignorance.

Marcus scoffs and crosses his arms. "Don't give me that. The noble sheriff Wallace is using his daughter as a punching bag. I know it. You know it. And I heard some other shit about what he's doing."

"Heard from where?" I'm asking in an even tone, but I can feel my pulse accelerating in excitement. Could this kid really have something useful that could help the case?

"If I tell you, I don't want any of this shit tied to me. I won't be giving any official statements or anything. This is just to help Jenny."

"This conversation is off the books." I wave my hand in acknowledgment. "You have my promise that it stays between us if it's something that can help clear Jennifer's name."

Marcus eyes me suspiciously and then nods before leaning closer to lower his voice. "I take part in a certain illegal activity..."

"How illegal are we talking?"

"Jesus, man. That's beside the point. The thing is, I know some people. You could call them a gang. They supply me with some things to distribute, if you catch my drift." He casts me a meaningful look, and I lift my chin in acknowledgment.

I'm not surprised to learn that this shithead is dealing. The guy has a certain look about him. What was Jen seeing in him, I wonder.

"So, yesterday I heard something I probably shouldn't, and from what I gathered, Wallace is mixed into some gun trafficking business with those guys. The thing that might interest you is that there's supposed to be a drop this afternoon at that abandoned warehouse by the river."

"That's it?"

"What the fuck do you mean that's it? Do you know how much I risk coming to the station and ratting out the people I work for? If they catch a whiff, I will be fucking staked. And that's not a metaphor, these guys ain't playing."

"Should've thought about it before you started dealing with a gang," I reply grimly.

"Fuck you!" Marcus jumps up from his seat, his face twisted in anger. "I only came here because I thought you getting Wallace will help Jenny. But maybe I shouldn't have bothered. Fucking cops!"

He moves to the door, but I stop him. "How sure are you about this tip?"

"Pretty fucking sure. I know what I heard." Marcus spits out and then hesitates, something weird flashing in his eyes. "Will you check it out?"

"Probably," I admit, and stand up from my desk to extend a hand for Marcus to shake it. "Thank you for your help, Marcus. I appreciate it."

He looks at my hand and then his gaze hardens before he shakes it. "Yeah. Later." And then he's out the door.

I stand with my hands on my hips and consider my next move. I'm not sure if I can trust that rat, but I have to admit that it's my only lead for now when it comes to David Wallace. For the last week, I've been trying to figure out how to help Jen, but I always come up empty. The only thing keeping me sane is the thought of her being under the safe care of my aunt.

My supervisors at the FBI were of no help, of course. After I had no other option than to report my involvement with Wallace's daughter's escape, admitting having jeopardized almost the whole investigation, they started to consider pulling me out completely of the job. The jury is still out, but I wouldn't exactly blame them. I fucked up, and I've been fucking up even more ever since I got to Bell Ridge. Maybe I'm burned out. Maybe I'm not cut out to be an agent.

After serving for six years in the Marines, I had no idea what to do with myself, and then a friend told me about a position in the agency. I thought it would be perfect for me. Using my training and knowledge to do something good for my country once again but more locally. Boy, was I wrong. The fucking bureaucracy, the rat race, the caring about what's more profitable for someone on the higher level than about the actual people and cases. It's frustrating and there's never any reward. Just the same bullshit over and over again.

Perhaps that's why I'm putting on my jacket and marching out before I can talk myself out of it or make the necessary calls, like I was trained. Instead I walk toward Diaz's desk and pull him aside to tell him where I'm going.

"Brody, you're crazy, man. You want to go there on your own to... do what exactly?"

"I'll just stake the place out, look around, maybe find out something useful and be back. I don't intend to engage. But if I spend one more day sitting on my ass and doing paperwork for Wallace so he can run around doing god knows what, I'm gonna lose my freaking mind. I need to start acting. Also, I'm armed and have you as a backup."

"Oh, great. I'm the backup," Diaz grumbles sarcastically, but puts on his jacket. "Let's go then."

I tap him on the shoulder in gratitude, and together we get out of the station with an excuse of getting some lunch before packing into my car.

• • • •

"ARE YOU SURE THAT MARCUS kid wasn't just pulling your leg?" Diaz asks after we spend two hours observing the warehouse from afar. So far, there's nothing happening and not a soul is in sight, but Marcus didn't give me a specific hour for the drop-off. Still, I would suspect someone keeping an eye on the place. For now, it's eerily quiet. Maybe they're hiding inside.

"I'm going to get closer to see if there's something in there," I say to the man crouching next to me behind the dilapidated fence.

"Don't think it's wise, Brody. There's an open field around the building. If someone's in there, they're gonna spot you right away."

"Yeah. But I'm done with sitting on my ass, remember? Stay here. I'm going to take a look and be back. If things go sideways, get the fuck out and call for backup."

"I thought I was the fucking backup," Diaz argues warily.

"The other backup, meaning the FBI, okay?" I pull a card from my pocket and hand it to him. "Call them if there's more trouble."

"The FBI... of-fucking-course." Diaz eyes the card disbelievingly. "Couldn't you tell me before that you're with the feds?"

"Not really," I respond, not really paying attention to the conversation.

"I think you could've mentioned it before you dragged me here in the middle of nowhere to have a front-seat view of a gun trafficking gang dealing with our crazy ass sheriff, you asshole! This is way more serious than I thought."

"Calm down, Diaz. This doesn't change anything," I reason with him, but it's half-hearted, as I'm already thinking of the best way to get into the warehouse. I don't think there's anyone here, but better to be safe than sorry.

"The fuck it doesn't," my colleague mutters, but drops to a better position to watch me as I start creeping closer to the abandoned building.

I move slowly, checking my surroundings the whole time, the gravel crunching silently under my boots, but still not a peep from anywhere. It's when I come closer to the back wall that I hear muffled voices coming from the inside. How did they get here? Or have they been here all this time?

Moving closer to one of the small windows, I sneak a peek, but only make out two silhouettes in the dark room standing over a crate filled with something. From here, I can't make out what they're saying or what's inside so I turn around the corner to get a better look from some other angle. That's when a sharp pain registers at the back of my head, right before everything turns dark.

• • • •

I WAKE UP DISORIENTED, sporting a splitting headache, and try to lift my hand to check out the source of the agonizing pain, but blink my eyes wide open when I realize both of my arms are restrained. When I look down, I see that I'm strapped into a chair in the middle of the warehouse. My legs are tied to the chair as well.

"Oh, good, you're awake. I was worried a bit that you were hit too hard and wouldn't make it before we had a chance to talk."

I squint my eyes in the darkened room and ask, "Wallace?" I can feel blood oozing from the back of my head. Motherfucker, but that hurts.

A slow villain-like clapping resonates through the room and the sheriff himself steps into my line of sight.

"Hi there, nice for you to join me. I'm glad that good-for-nothing scum did his job. Wasn't sure about his ability to do the right thing, what's with him fucking that useless little whore that I've been calling my daughter, but surprisingly, he delivered. Good."

"You know who I am, right?" I ask with a sneer.

Wallace snorts contemptuously before spitting on the floor. "Fucking FBI. Sending undercover idiots onto my fucking turf. This is my fucking town. My rules!"

It's my turn to snort, but I soon regret the motion when a pulsating pain spreads through my head and I grimace.

"Anyway, I would probably never suspect a thing. I admit, I didn't think anyone would be ballsy enough to come and spy on me. Maybe, I would've even clued you in on the side business, and then I would be done." He laughs maniacally before continuing. "But you made a mistake. Oh, man, did you make one. You crossed me on the first day. You got interested in my family. Furthermore, you got interested in that little brat. So in return, I got interested in you."

The sheriff comes to crouch in front of the chair, and I start to struggle, yearning to wrap my hands around his throat.

"It was so fun watching you underestimate the power I have over my town. I've had people watching you constantly, reporting to me about your whereabouts and your secret meetings with Jennifer. I enjoyed watching you chase your tail for almost two years. But all good times must come to an end."

"Why the fuck are you still talking? If you want me dead, then fucking kill me before you annoy me to death with your self-praise," I spit through gritted teeth.

That makes Wallace cackle, and at this moment I can see that there's not a shred of reason in this guy's mind. He fucking lost it completely.

"Oh, I will kill you, but my boys still need to arrange a few things. You see, killing an FBI agent isn't something I want to go down for. So, we have to be a little creative here. Good thing, our business partner, so to speak, told us about troubles they had with their rivals. We'll kill two birds with one stone. Get rid of you and blame it on the enemy. A perfect solution."

"How do you know that I didn't already notify the FBI that I'm here?"

The maniac replies with a toothy smile. "Told you. I have eyes and ears everywhere. You did everything like you were supposed to. So predictable. Although, we are still looking for Diaz. We know he left the station with you."

"So you got that kid Marcus working for you?" I ask, changing the subject. If Diaz got out, then good for him. I'd rather talk to Dr. Evil here about his sinister scheme than have that man on my conscience.

"Not exactly. The information he fed you was mostly true. The boy did eavesdrop on a personal conversation. What he probably failed to mention, though, is the fact that he got caught. You see, I'm still the sheriff. And the kid was breaking the law and selling drugs. So, I only had to use a little persuasion to get him to do my dirty work."

"Persuasion? More like threatening," I grouse, my head lolling to the side involuntarily. Black spots appear in front of my eyes, and I blink them away before focusing on the man keeping me hostage.

"Yeah, I see you're getting weaker, I hope you will survive to witness the big finale. I want to see the look on your face." I frown and look up as he jumps up with glee. "Oh! Just in time."

Wallace swings my phone in front of my face and I can see that my aunt Ruth is calling. What is he playing at?

"This is going to be good." The sheriff waits for the call to switch to voicemail and then when the screen lights up to indicate the awaiting message, he clicks on it and plays it for me to hear.

"Damon," Ruth's distraught voice echoes in the building. "Why aren't you picking up, boy? I don't know what's going on, but the police came to take Jenny. They couldn't find her here, so I think she escaped, but I don't know if she managed to get away. Did you hear from her? Please, call me when you get this."

I feel nauseous when I look at Wallace's smirk in disbelief. "How the fuck did you track her?"

Once again he laughs and then tsks as if he's disappointed in me. "Track her? I knew exactly where she was the whole time. Again, so it gets through your thick skull, I have eyes everywhere in town. I know everything that happens around here. I was just biding my time and thinking of a way to get rid of you."

"Oh! Look, again, like clockwork!" Wallace lifts the phone and this time I can see that it's Jen calling me. "Such a shame you won't be there to rescue her. But don't worry, I will take over for you. At first, I didn't understand why you were all losing your heads over that ugly slut, but after the last time when I got my first feel of that sweet pussy, I have to admit she's got that something. Can't wait to dive right back in there," he taunts me with a sickening grin.

"You motherfucker!" I roar and start trashing in the chair, making it wobble, as Wallace laughs mockingly and licks his fingers in a vulgar way. "You're fucking dead! I'll fucking kill you!"

I struggle to get free, wanting to rip that fucker apart with my bare hands. What he's suggesting makes my blood feel like liquid lava under my skin, and for a moment, I don't feel weak. I don't feel the pain. I just see red. If I could just put my hands on him, I would pummel him to the ground, and no one would be able to tell what it was from his remains afterward.

"Boss! Everything's in place. The gang signs are in place. We're ready to go." One of the officers, Owens, comes in and spares me a quick glance with a grimace before looking away.

"Great!" Wallace drops my phone, making it shatter on the floor, and claps his hands once. "It was nice knowing you, Agent." He turns and marches away as he yells out, "Light it up, boys!"

Two unknown men walk in with cans and start pouring from them alongside every wall. Don't have to be a genius to guess it's gasoline. They do their job without acknowledging me, even as I begin to struggle so hard that the chair gives up on me and I fall to the floor.

"Fuck!" I hiss and try to see if I can get any part of the chair to break, but it's pointless, even for somebody my size.

The two goons walk out, and I hear a sharp whistle outside before a wild-spreading fire envelopes the whole warehouse within two seconds.

Great, I'm going to die here, and it's all thanks to my own stupidity and hotheadedness.

The growing flames start climbing the walls and encircle me completely from all sides. My throat starts burning from the heavy smoke I inhale with each breath. Before I will myself to try getting the ties loose on my arms again, I hear faint sounds of footsteps and coughing and squint to see what's happening around me. Diaz runs in my direction, trying to avoid the blazing fire with a jacket wrapped around his mouth and nose.

"Run, you stupid asshole!" I seethe, but he doesn't listen, just runs up and starts cutting the ties with his pocketknife hastily. His hands are shaking.

When I'm freed from the chair, I roll over and try to get to my feet, but lose balance and almost topple over. I'm quickly pulled by my arm and together with Diaz we shuffle to the exit.

Suddenly, a loud boom reaches my ear and I feel something slam into the right side of my chest. The burning piece of wood that fell from the ceiling scorches my skin, and I instinctively push it away before dropping to my knees with an agonized roar, pulling Diaz down with me.

"Come on, man. We're almost out." Diaz's muffled voice is pleading. I look into his scared eyes, and I know I can't be responsible for making orphans out of this guy's kids. So with the last remains of strength, I pull myself up once again and stumble out before the roof collapses. I land on the ground and start coughing, my whole body is trembling and in shock. My right shoulder and pec reek with the smell of burned flesh.

Diaz crouches next to me and then falls on his ass just as FBI cars start pulling in, the firetruck right behind them.

"They took their fucking time," I croak in between coughs.

"Yeah, didn't take me seriously at first. Took me time to present the entire situation since you didn't let in anyone on your genius plan," Diaz wheezes and glances at me before refocusing on the people running around and feds making calls. I see an ambulance pull up with the corner of my eye, when he continues, "Do me a favor, Brody."

"Anything, man," I grunt right away and try to keep my need to cough in check.

"If you pull through, leave, I don't want to ever see you again," Diaz states with a serious face.

"You got it," I reply, and then my eyes roll before I promptly pass out.

CHAPTER VI

Jenny
The whole week in the women's shelter seemed unreal to me.

From the moment I woke up the next day after Brody left me here, I felt like I was thrown into a parallel universe where most people are genuinely kind and don't have a hidden agenda.

As far as my memory goes, my life always consisted of instability and hostile adults. Well, maybe my mother wasn't hostile, but she always looked the other way when I was being pummeled to the ground. It took me coming here and meeting all the fierce women, who are running away from their monsters, many with small children, to finally realize something. When standing by and pretending all was well, my mother was my abuser too. At least in a way. She contributed to the violence simply by normalizing it, never saying stop or even trying to change our situation.

Most mothers here fought tooth and nail for their children, to get them out, and to give them a better life. When listening to some stories, I couldn't help but ask myself, "Didn't my mother love me enough to protect me? Why was she okay with everything that was happening?"

The first two days here, I spent half the time lying in bed staring at the ceiling and doing small chores around the place, mostly keeping to myself.

By the third day, I was approached by a redhead named Lucy, who had been eyeing me curiously ever since I came down for breakfast the first morning. She was so open and lively, reminding me a little of Claire, so I decided to come out of my shell a bit. We struck up an easy conversation right away, and it turned out we have a lot in common when it comes to favorite music and movies.

Lucy's been here since last month and is hiding away from an ex-boyfriend who stalked her daily and then broke into her apartment. She called the police and got a restraining order, but they couldn't do much to ensure her safety, so when she started to receive threats in her mail, she ran. It wouldn't be long before she came upon Ruth's shelter for battered women.

On the next day, I met a woman named Amelia, who has two little daughters, named Sammy and Silvia. She's been running away from her husband for a while now. Before Amelia decided to leave her abusive husband, she used to work as a cook's helper at a restaurant, so Aunt Ruth offered her a job at the shelter and has given her and her daughters their own room.

From what I've got, they've been living here for a year. Amelia seems to be one of the gentlest souls I have ever met in my life, and I can't imagine a situation in which someone wants to hurt her. Not that the rest of us deserve it, but she's just so sweet and kind. Her piece of shit husband had to do a number on her. She rarely leaves the building and if she has an errand to run, she needs to have someone with her because interacting with men or even being around one scares her so much she freaks out.

I know all of this from Lucy, who went into a supermarket with Amelia two weeks ago, and there was some incident involving a male cashier.

The other women seem to be coming and going through the shelter, each of them welcomed with open arms by Ruth, who doesn't ask any questions. She never comments on anyone's bruises or asks for their story. Just always stays ready with her reassuring smile.

Many girls come for the night, seeking a safe place to sleep, and in the morning they are out without a word. At first, I was baffled by that revolving door of women coming and going whenever they find it convenient. Then Ruth told me that we don't know what others are going through and that she's happy to provide them with at least one peaceful night in a safe environment.

She also informed me that some of them will come back here, and sadly, some of them will go back to their tormentors. But there will be those who recover and move on. From what I gathered, Ruth sees the shelter as a sort of interchange station for most women, waiting here until they leave for their next destination.

Maybe she's right. I've been here for a week now and that's exactly what I'm doing. Waiting for my next step. Checking my phone constantly, willing Brody to tell me what to do now.

"If you stare any harder at that thing, it's going to catch on fire," Lucy teases as she comes into the room carrying a plastic bag.

I drop the ever-silent phone on the bed next to me and sigh, "Not that I don't like it here, but I can't exactly sit on my ass until someone else figures my shit out. I have no family and no plan. And I miss my friend Claire. This sucks."

Lucy plops down next to me and nudges me with her shoulder. "Cheer up, Sunshine. Ruth will let you stay here for as long as you want. I didn't figure out my shit yet too and I've been here longer. It's good to take a breather before you start over."

"Yeah, but that's the thing, though. What does starting over even mean? I can't imagine my life back at Bell Ridge, even without my father in it. And I also can't imagine leaving it all behind. Do I even trust the system after everything? I feel like everything Brody told me is just his wishful thinking. It's a fucking mess." I hang my head and massage my temples, already feeling the oncoming headache.

"Jenny, you need to chill. You stressing over it isn't going to bring you any answers. What you need to do is distance yourself a little from it, and focus on yourself, and your healing. I'm sure everything else will fall into place."

"I guess you're right," I muse and nod toward the bag swinging between Lucy's knees. "So, what's in the bag?"

She lifts it with a shit-eating grin and exclaims, "A makeover!"

"A what?" I ask, confused.

"I was wondering how I can help you get out of this funk you seem to be stuck in. And I thought what better to cheer a girl up than a new haircut? I went to the store and got some hair dye and scissors." Lucy starts taking out items from the bag excitedly.

I lean away from her and put my arms up in a defensive gesture. "Are you crazy? Have you seen my hair? You would need a tanker full of dye to color all this," I point toward my crazy curls.

"That's why I bought extra," Lucy singsongs. "And I really think the change will do you some good. Other than that, it's a perfect way to disguise yourself. Do you think I'm a natural redhead?"

I eye her hair slowly. She's got a point, but I would rather not end up looking like a freak. My hair was always a touchy subject for me, wild, thick, and curly, the color somewhere between brown and auburn. It was always impossible to tame it, so I've just given up on it. I want to avoid adding a bad dye job to it.

"Okay. But you know what you're doing, right?"

"Of course!" Lucy waves her hand. "I've been doing it forever. I have two sisters, and we used to dye each other's hair constantly. Trust me, you will look fab!"

"All right then, let's do it." I rise from the bed and laugh when Lucy jumps up after me with a happy squeal.

• • • •

"SOOO, WHAT DO YOU THINK?" Lucy asks insecurely, biting her lip, as she's holding the mirror up.

I eye my new look critically in the bathroom and keep a straight face for as long as I can, then explode, "I fucking love it!"

Lucy exhales loudly with one hand on her chest. "Jesus, I thought you were going to hate me."

Laughing earnestly for the first time since I came here, I hug her and say, "No, it's truly great. Did you think about doing it for a living? Really, you've got talent, Lucy." I move closer to the mirror to inspect my new haircut again.

My hair is now dyed light blonde. Lucy shortened it a bit with scissors, so now they don't even reach my shoulders, and then straightened it with a flat iron. The whole look is completed by delicate side-swept bangs. Honestly, I look good. And not like me at all. I honestly have trouble recognizing myself right now. Claire would freak out if she saw this.

"Oh, it's nothing. And you have great natural hair. I would kill to have that volume. Anyway, the aim was to help you start the new chapter or whatever. Also, you look almost unrecognizable, so that's a bonus if your father was looking for you or something."

At the mention of my dad, I flinch involuntarily, but try not to let it show as I smile. "Yeah, thank you again for doing this."

"Don't mention it," Lucy chirps and links our arms together, turning us toward the door. "Now, it's almost lunchtime. I wonder what Amelia prepared today. I hope..."

Lucy gets cut off as the door to the bathroom opens suddenly and Amelia falls through it, looking as if a horde of demons was chasing her, breathing erratically, her eyes wide open.

"Amelia? What's wrong?" Lucy entangles herself from me and runs toward the frightened woman.

Amelia completely ignores her though as her big eyes focus only on me. "The men, they're here," she pants.

"What men?" I'm too stunned to speak, so Lucy asks for me.

"The police, they came here looking for you, Jenny. Ruth is trying to stop them, but they have a warrant. It won't be long until they come upstairs. She sent me here to tell you, you have to run. They will come here." She shudders.

We're all turning our heads in synchronization toward the open door when we hear multiple masculine voices coming from the staircase. Lucy immediately jumps forward and closes the door, locking it with a key.

"That will hold them off, but you have to run, Jenny. You're a minor and the police will release you straight to your father's hands."

I look frantically around the stalls and bathroom sinks. "What?! Where do you want me to go? Do you have a fucking Chamber of Secrets tucked somewhere in here or something?"

"Don't be ridiculous!" Lucy hisses and moves from the door to the window and opens it to look down. "You'll have to jump."

"We're on the second floor, I'll break my fucking legs!" I clip back, but then hear the voices getting closer, and I know my time is running out.

"There's a dumpster right by the wall, try to land in it," Lucy whispers urgently and gives me a quick hug.

"W-what about my things? I only h-have my phone with me," I stutter as the door knob starts to jiggle and Amelia lets out a scared whimper, moving away from the door.

"Call your guy! He's with the law, I'm sure he'll be right on his way," Lucy tries to reassure me in a calm voice, but by the look on her face, I can see that she's truly freaked out by the whole situation.

We all jump up when there is a loud knock on the door. "Police! Open up!"

"Shit," I mutter and glance at Amelia who looks like she's about to pass out and then nod to Lucy one last time before lifting myself over the window seal.

I look down and gulp loudly before moving a little to the right, so I have a better chance of landing in the trash two levels down. I say a fast prayer in my mind and then jump.

Whoever came up with the idea of fleeing heroes in movies falling softly on bags of trash and then getting up and running as if nothing ever happened, has probably never experienced anything like it. Because this shit fucking hurts. I groan in pain and curse under my nose as I try to get up. My body barely had a chance to heal this last week, and now the whole process has to start again.

What are people throwing out? Fucking bricks?

Knowing I don't have much time because if the cops won't find me in the building, they will search around the area, I pull myself to my feet and climb out of the large container. I ignore the pain in my leg and limp toward the back alley.

I walk for maybe around thirty minutes, turning into random streets, looking over my shoulder constantly, and hiding my face with my hair as a police patrol drives right past me, before finding a bench in a shady-looking neighborhood. Plopping down breathless and sweaty, I take out my phone from the pocket of my jeans, happy that the small device and I became inseparable the last week. Right now, it's my only lifeline.

I look at the screen and am a little alarmed when I don't see any missed calls from Brody waiting there. I would have thought Ruth had already called him to tell him what's happened and that he'd be searching for me.

Taking a deep breath, I click on his number and curse when the signal rings and rings until the answering machine picks up to ask me to leave a message. I dial again and this time the machine picks up right away. Oh, no. Please, God, tell me he didn't turn off his phone. I try with the same effect and then try again.

I'm to the point of hysterics when I see the battery on my phone is almost dead. Grabbing my new hair, I tug on it and say, "Fuck it all to shit."

Leaning back on the bench, I look up at the sky and shudder. I rub my arms, trying to keep warm as the temperature slowly drops.

What do I do now? Was Brody just talking out of his ass the whole time and didn't give a shit in reality?

And the more important question, how did my father even find me here? I thought my situation couldn't get more fucked up.

I thought I touched rock bottom last week. Yet, I was wrong. So, so wrong. It can always get worse because now I have no money, no clothes, and no roof over my head. And to make matters worse, I'm still searched by the police for things I didn't even do. Well mostly, if you don't count the stealing part, which turned out to be all for nothing anyway as everything was in my bag that stayed at the shelter.

I think about at least trying to get back there to collect them, but then quickly decide against it. It's too risky to show my face there so soon, and truth be told, I don't know if I would be even able to find the place right now. I didn't keep count of the streets I passed. I don't even know in what part of Madison I am at.

My heart jumps in my throat when my phone pings with a notification and I scramble quickly to unlock it, thinking it may be a message from Brody. A heartbroken wail almost leaves my lips when I see it's just the device informing me it's in need of a charger, with only five percent to spare.

I look at the last sunbeams disappearing behind buildings and breathe out slowly before trying one last time. When the answering machine picks up again, I close my eyes, willing the tears to stop.

After the beep, I clear my throat and say, "Hey, Brody. If you're hearing this, you probably already know that I had to run. I'll be fine, though. I just wanted..." My voice breaks, so I try again. "I just wanted to say thank you for getting me out and trying to help, even if not everything worked out. I'll never forget your kindness."

I swap angrily at the lonely tear that escaped before continuing. "I have one last request, though. If you run into Claire by any chance, could you please tell her not to worry about me? And tell her that I love her and that being friends with her was the best thing that ever happened to me." I choke on my tears before I can get the last part out. "Goodbye, Brody."

The call ends just before the screen goes blank, and I throw the phone into the nearest garbage can.

I sit back down and break into uncontrollable tears, crying my heart out for all the unfairness of the world. When will I catch a fucking break? I'm seventeen years old, for fuck's sake. I should be sitting at Claire's, gossiping about boys, watching shitty horror movies, and talking smack about our teachers. Not become a homeless criminal on a run from her deranged father.

"Hey, are you all right?" A masculine voice pulls me out of my pity party, and I look up to find three guys standing there and giving me measuring looks. Two of them look quite scary but the one in the middle, who, I'm assuming, is the one who asked, wears a concerned expression on his face.

I sniffle and straighten up from my hunched position. "I got... lost."

The two threatening men snort, but the nicer-looking one steps further and asks, "Do you need help? I'm Ricky and these two are Alto and Churro." He points at each of his companions, introducing them. "And what's your name, beautiful?"

I hesitate before going with the truth, "Jenny."

"Jenny," Ricky tastes the name on his lips and smiles coyly before bowing his head slightly. "It's a pleasure to meet you, Jenny. Now, I'm not a man who likes to watch pretty girls cry. Sitting on their own in a neighborhood like this. This is not a good place to get lost in, little Jenny."

I narrow my eyes at him and stand up, ignoring the way Ricky's eyes survey my body. "I didn't ask for your opinion, Ricky. And you don't exactly choose a place in which you get lost. That's fucking stupid."

Ricky's smile stretches wider. "Oh, I like you, Jenny."

I roll my eyes and deadpan, "Glad you approve. But I couldn't care less."

Ricky laughs and ignores my comment. "Tell you what, the guys and I were just going to get some food. Why don't you join us, and later we can hang out, have some beers, and chill together."

"Does chilling together require taking off my clothes?" I ask dryly, ready to get away from here.

Again, the man laughs and looks at me like I'm the funniest creature in the world. "Not if you don't want to. When I say chill, I mean chill. And it doesn't look like you have anywhere else to be at the moment. So," he claps his hands once. "Are you coming, Jenny?"

"Why would I go anywhere with strangers?" I ask and rub my shoulders.

"Darling, we're not exactly strangers. We came over and introduced ourselves, so you already know who we are." He waves his hand, gesturing around the street. "It's the others that are strangers, and I can't exactly promise you that they will all be as friendly as us."

I look around and am surprised to discover how many shady-looking people are lurking around the dark street. While I was having my meltdown, I got surrounded and didn't even notice it. I make eye contact with some dude standing with a bottle. He takes a sip as he leans on one of the buildings and eyes me hungrily, instantly giving me the creeps.

"Shit," I mumble under my breath.

Great, this is fantastic. Right now, it seems I have three options.

Option one, turn on my heel and run toward the nearest police station to give myself up. That means I will soon be back at my house with my lovely father, being beaten and most probably raped.

Option two, I stay here waiting for a miracle to happen and get kidnapped and most likely raped by some creep.

Option three, I go with Ricky and his friends, and get food and a place to wait for a while where I can also most likely get raped. But there's also a chance they'll be alright.

Some options I have.

The chilly air around me, my growling stomach, and the death of the last shreds of hope for some miracle to save me, are what makes the decision for me. After all, desperate times call for desperate measures.

"Let's go then," I announce to Ricky, to which he smiles triumphantly before leading the way.

CHAPTER VII

J enny – 21 years old

Boom, boom, boom. I feel the bass vibrating through the floor, as my head lolls to the side. I look up, and then quickly shut my eyes when the blurred lights assault my stinging eyeballs. I try to touch my aching head, but my arms feel too heavy to lift.

"Hey, there, little Jenny. Having fun?"

The image whirls after I'm being yanked up, and now I'm drunkenly dancing in a crowded, stuffy room full of strangers. I pull my hands up, gyrating my hips to the rhythm. When I feel a tap on my shoulder, I twirl around.

"Ricky!" I throw myself at the smiling man, almost knocking us both to the ground in the process.

"Hey, girl. Been looking for you all over the place," Ricky yells to my ear, and nods at his outstretched hand with two white pills on it.

"What is it?" I ask, slurring my words.

"Does it matter?" He shrugs.

The scenery changes yet again, and now I sit on the floor, my legs fully exposed, so I peer down with a frown to realize that I'm only wearing my underwear. I hiss in surprise when I feel stinging pain in my fingers as the cigarette I didn't even know I was holding, starts burning out.

"Motherfucker," I flick the butt and brush off the ash from my fingers.

I hear a squeak of a mattress, and look around to find the source of the sound, narrowing my eyes at the half-naked man coming toward me.

"Wow, you're a wild one, little Jenny." Ricky's friend Churro laughs before walking out. I cringe and shiver at the realization of what he's implicating before standing up on unsteady legs.

Then I notice Ricky's body, still sleeping soundly, naked on the bed. Our clothes and empty bottles are thrown around him, like a hurricane of depravity swiped through the whole room.

I walk up to him and tug on his arm impatiently, my whole body shaking as it starts sobering up.

"Ricky, wake up! I need something. Where's the stuff?" I question frantically and look around, hoping to spot some leftover zip lock bag.

"Ricky, wake, the fuck, up!"

"Wake up!"

I wake with a start, my alarm blaring in the still-dark room. I don't think I will ever get used to waking up at five. Whoever came up with the idea of starting their day before six should be burning in hell for all eternity.

"Shut the fuck up," I grumble at the annoying device before slapping it with my hand, probably harder than necessary, but I went to bed late last night and ended up tossing and turning for two hours before I was able to fall asleep.

"What the fuck?" I grouse when I sit on the edge of the bed and my bare feet touch the icy cold floor.

Please don't tell me the heater broke again because right now, I don't think we can even afford groceries for this week. I move through the room and snatch a sweater I discarded at the foot of the bed yesterday to put it on my shivering body before I exit my bedroom.

The smell of coffee mixed with cigarette smoke welcomes me as I enter the kitchen, where Rita is already sitting at the table and scrolling on her phone, looking fully awake. If she feels the cold, she doesn't show it.

"It's cold as a witch's tit in here. The heating broke or something?" I ask Rita and pour myself a cup of strong coffee. I sigh in contentment after taking the first sip as I wait for her to finally acknowledge me.

"How the fuck should I know? Move your useless ass for once and go check it," she mumbles without looking up.

I give her the stink eye but don't comment. Rita may be a bitch, but she still allowed me to live here and found me a job. So even though we don't exactly see eye to eye, I still am grateful for her. Or at least try to be because the old hag is making it really difficult sometimes.

Taking my cup with me, I go to the basement to check on the heater and release a string of curses when I see the small screen informing me that there is no gas supply available.

"Fucking bitch," I curse in a low voice.

I run back into the kitchen and slap both hands on the table in front of the older woman. "What did you do with the money I gave you to pay the gas bill?"

Rita looks up at me, one of her eyebrows making its way up, wrinkling her face even more than it already is. Maybe she was beautiful once upon a time. But age gracefully, she did not.

"I gave it to Ricky. He called that he needed help, so I sent him some," Rita declares and ignores the angry hiss I give out at the news.

"Well, congratulations, Rita. Because now it's fucking freezing in here!" I thunder and slam my hand on the table again, making it shake.

"Really? I don't feel anything. Aren't you a bit dramatic?" She stares back at me with an unimpressed face before lighting up another cigarette.

"Oh, I guess you're right, I'm sorry. I actually can't feel anything," I start in a fake melodic voice and then snap at her. "Because my toes went fucking numb from the cold floors!"

Rita tsks and shakes her head in irritation, blowing smoke through her mouth. "I don't know what my son ever saw in you. You're an ungrateful brat if I ever saw one. Now stop whining, and maybe put on some clothes instead of running around half-naked and complaining about the cold. And get a fucking move on, you're gonna be late."

"Whatever," I grumble and turn away before throwing off my shoulder. "And what did I tell you about smoking in the house?"

"Last time I checked it was still my house, so I will smoke wherever the fuck I want," she clips back.

I huff in anger and rush to change into my waitress uniform, cursing Rita silently under my breath the whole time.

Then I move to the small room adjoining my bedroom and tiptoe toward the small crib, where I find my sweet baby boy still sleeping. I take an extra blanket and cover him, hoping he won't notice the temperature drop around him.

As usual, a soft smile overtakes my face as I look at the only reason I'm still here among the living. Even though my baby came as a complete surprise to me, and I was definitely too young to become a mother, undoubtedly he gave me a sense of purpose. He became the only family I will ever need.

I kiss my son on his soft forehead and sigh. I hate leaving him for the day with his grandmother, but because I became a single mother at barely nineteen, there's not much choice for me in this department. There aren't many people I would trust with my baby, and Rita may be this smoking like a chimney, rude bitch that hates my guts, but she actually loves her grandson. And she's watching him for free, so I won't lie that it wasn't a big factor in the decision to let her babysit for me.

Checking the time, I curse and get a move on before my boss bites my head off for being late again. After I rush into the bathroom to brush my teeth and pull my hair into a messy bun on the top of my head, I glance quickly at my reflection and grimace. I may be twenty-one years old, but I look worn out and ugly already.

I was always super skinny, but after everything went down with Ricky, I lost a few pounds I didn't have to spare. My hair grew out, and I never had the heart, or the money, to go to a hair salon to recreate the look Lucy had given me three years ago. My eyes stand out even more in my sullen-looking face, sporting dark circles underneath.

Shaking my head at myself, I get out of the bathroom searching for my apron and then run back to the living room.

"Henry is still sleeping. I gave him a blanket, so I hope he won't catch a cold," I mutter in annoyance in Rita's direction.

"The boy will be fine. A little cold won't kill him. Stop bitching about it," I get in response.

I take a deep breath to calm down. After living alone with Rita for over a year, I know it's better to choose my battles wisely.

"Anyway, I'll probably be back later today since I need to go to the bank after work and try to solve the issue." I collect my bag and my phone, and pin Rita with an insistent look.

"And don't smoke close to Henry. All we need is for him to get asthma."

"Pshh, you, lecturing me? That's rich. As if I don't know how to raise a boy," the woman says.

"Do you?" I ask sarcastically and get out before Rita can curse me out.

I march toward my car, looking around and checking my surroundings. This neighborhood hasn't changed much since I started living here. Yes, many people know me now and associate me with Ricky, who grew up here and knows everyone. But it's still a dangerous place.

Turning the key in the ignition of my piece of shit car, I pray for it to start because I'm already running late for work. Finally, after the third try, the car splutters to life and I peel out of the parking lot.

· · · ·

"TOOK YOU LONG ENOUGH, princess," is the first thing I hear from my boss, Gary, as I step foot into the diner I'm serving at.

I scratch nervously behind my ear. "I'm sorry, Gary. My heater broke down again, I had to deal with it."

He eyes me and huffs in annoyance, "Right. Just don't make it a habit. It's the second time this week that you're late."

"It won't happen again," I promise and then frown at his retreating form as he grumbles to himself about unreliable employees.

Shit, I need to be more careful. If I lose my job now, we're screwed. With Rita constantly sending over all of her pension to her son, and with me barely being able to save any money with my minimum wage job, we're on the verge of being completely broke.

Wanting to appease my grumpy boss, I quickly get to work. Soon enough, I find myself in sync with the whole place and enjoying the smooth workflow.

I never thought I'd say this, but I actually like my job as a waitress. If you can ignore grabby assholes and some nasty comments, this work can be pretty bearable. Most people leave nice tips if you serve them right, and I get free food if we have some leftovers. Also, apart from today, Gary can be a really cool and understanding boss. He can be a big softy, unless you cross him. And he knows I have a two-year-old at home, and is always trying to adjust the schedule to my conditions. The only thing that really irks him is not being here on time, and I'm on strike two right now.

Trying to make up for my earlier screw-up, I move my ass faster than usual and concentrate fully on my tasks, letting the hours pass me by. When the time for my break comes, I grab my sandwich and eat it in a hurry in the backroom, instead of taking my time at the back steps of the diner as usual. I use the rest of the time to clean the tables and make myself useful, in the hope that Gary acknowledges my effort and doesn't get rid of me the next time I come in late.

After my shift ends I feel beat and tired, and I am dreaming about a hot shower, knowing that if I don't deal with the gas company and pay the bill soon, I won't be getting any hot water today. I exit the diner through the back door, waving my goodbye to my boss, who already seemed to forget about this morning, as he waves back with a warm smile on his face.

I hurry to my car, trying to decide which route I need to take to get to the bank before it closes, when I almost stumble at the sight of two men in police uniforms stepping onto my path.

It has been a long time since I stopped sweating every time a police cruiser passed me by on the street, or when officers knocked on my door. Living with Ricky has changed my approach to law enforcement a little. Instead of worrying about my father sending someone to get me, each time I encountered the police, I wondered what my idiot baby daddy did this time. Yet, the way both men eye me makes me instantly apprehensive now.

"Are you Jennifer Wallace?" one of them asks.

Stopping a few feet from them, I answer with an unnecessarily hostile voice, "Depends on who's asking."

"I'm Officer Walken," the older of the two takes out his badge to show me and then motions to his companion. "This is Officer Rusoe. Are you Jennifer Wallace?"

I glance at his badge and swallow, before taking a step closer to take a look at the presented item.

Peering back at the man, I respond with, "Yes. What's this about?"

The younger policeman steps forward and replies politely, "Ma'am, if you could follow us to the station. We have been ordered to bring you for questioning as a witness."

"Am I in trouble?" I inquire slowly.

"Miss, we would just like to talk to you about a case you've been a part of. We would rather not do it on the street, but really it is up to you. You could follow us, then after all is done you'll be on your way," the one called Walken says matter-of-factly.

"All right," I agree reluctantly. "Lead the way."

. . . .

I SIT IN ONE OF THE investigation rooms, getting impatient when the door opens and in walks the younger officer from before.

"Sorry we've kept you waiting, Miss Wallace. Now that Detective Barnett is here, we can start."

Said detective walks in with some files under his armpit and a coffee cup in his other hand. His forehead wrinkles in a frown as he sits opposite of me and peruses me quickly.

Do I have something on my face? I fight the need to swipe at my mouth and concentrate back on the man. He looks a little familiar, but I can't quite put my finger on where I saw him before. But I feel like I know those eyes. Bizarre.

The man seems to shake himself quickly of whatever got him unsettled and clears his throat before slapping the folder on the table, "Thank you for coming in. I'm Detective Barnett, and you already know Officer Rusoe. I have to say it wasn't easy to find you, Miss... can I call you Jennifer?"

"I guess..." I mutter and then look at my watch. "Look, like I told the police before, whatever Ricky allegedly did before he went to jail, I had no part in it whatsoever..."

"If you're talking about your boyfriend Enrique Rodriguez, he's not the reason you are here today," the detective answers and shifts in his seat.

"Ex-boyfriend," I correct automatically. "And he's not? Then what's this about?" I ask, but already have a feeling where this is going. Shit. I knew this wouldn't be the end of it. What the hell was I thinking? That my father will just let it go?

"When was the last time you saw your mother, Marissa Wallace?" he asks in an even tone, but his eyes seem sad.

"I..." I scratch my head nervously and lick my lips. "I haven't seen my mother in three years. The last time we spoke was the day I ran away from my house," I admit and blink up at both men, wondering where this is headed.

The detective flips the case file open and nods, "Yes, we have it all in here. Runaway, accused of assaulting both of your parents and of stealing family savings from your father's office. But that's not what happened, is it?"

I shake my head vehemently and pin the man with a serious expression. "I thought that Bell Ridge police had already established that I was the one being assaulted. When I contacted them like two years ago, they told me the case was long closed..." When the man continues to stare at me, I continue forcefully, "I was forced to leave my own home because I was scared for my life, and everything I've done back then was to save myself. I honestly don't think I would be alive right now if I didn't leave."

Again the detective nods as if my words are confirming what he already knew or predicted for me to say, then in a matter of few words he destroys my world when he says solemnly, "It hurts me to say this, Jennifer, but we found your mother's body last week. We suspect she might have been dead for over two years."

The man continues to speak, but all I hear are bits and pieces, his mouth is moving at a normal pace, but the words seem to flow to me in weird slow motion. I make out the words "strangled" and "basement" before I blink rapidly, forcing my mind to cooperate.

"... the investigation. Of course, considering everything that happened in the past, David Wallace is our main suspect for the moment. We hoped that maybe you'll be willing to share some light on your parents' relationship, it could help us understand his motives better..."

"Wait," I cut in shakily, making Detective Barnett look up at me in question. "I don't understand how she could be dead for two years, and it's just now that you found her. Was no one concerned when she disappeared? I mean... like the neighbors or something?"

The detective shares a confused look with the police officer, who's been taking notes of everything that was being said until now, and it's the younger man who answers me with a frown. "When the sheriff's actions came to light after the fire at the warehouse in Bell Ridge, he took your mother with him and fled. The Madison Police Department took over the investigation with the support of the FBI, since it involved gun and drug trafficking, and we've been searching for your father ever since."

I squint at the man, completely stupefied, and look to Detective Barnett for confirmation.

"Recently, we got a lead on his whereabouts, and went to check it," the younger man continues. "We didn't find David Wallace in there, but it was clear that it was his hiding place for some time. It wasn't until we got to the basement that we discovered the decomposed body of a woman, we couldn't recognize her..."

"Officer, that's enough," Barnett grouses, when I start to pant, feeling the blood draining from my face. "Could you wait outside? I'd like to question Jennifer privately."

"Yeah. Sure. I'm sorry for your loss, Miss Wallace," the police officer says regretfully and exits the room.

I breathe through my mouth to calm myself down, but then cover it when a wail tries to escape me.

"I'm so sorry about that. Rusoe is still a rookie, and gets excited about the job, which can come off as insensitive... Would you like me to bring you something to drink?" the older guy asks quietly.

It takes me a second to pull myself together, and I shake my head before I straighten in my seat. I want to get it over with and go back home.

Now that it's just us in the room, the man sitting across from me gets rid of his professional detective mask as he sighs heavily and drags a hand across his tired face.

Once again I notice how familiar his sad eyes look, and I have to ask, "Do I know you from somewhere? I feel like we've met before."

His eyebrows lift in surprise before he looks to the side, "I don't think so. But I knew your parents. We've been friends back in the day..."

My eyes widen at the man when a realization hits me. "You're that Robert. Robert Barnett."

The man looks taken aback by the fact that I heard about him and doesn't respond, so I continue, "Mom told me about you. She said that you were in the military with my father."

"Did your mom... say anything else?" Robert seems uncomfortable as he asks in a low voice.

Seeing how flustered he is at the thought that I might know about their affair back in the day makes me shake my head in negation, and I notice the way he breathes in relief.

"So how did you end up leading this case? Isn't this some kind of conflict of interests or something if you and David were friends?" I ask to preoccupy my mind with something before I shatter. I can feel the grief trying to swallow me, but I need to put it aside for the moment. I need to know what happened.

Happy with the subject change, Detective Barnett returns to his professional mode. "Obviously I can't share every detail of the investigation with you, but the fact was, your father wanted to expand his business all the way to Madison. He wanted to enter the game against some bigger players, so to speak. For that, he needed someone trusted here..."

"Risky," I mutter.

Robert nods before continuing, "We kept in touch throughout the years, but I wouldn't say at that point that we were best friends. Anyway, during our meeting he was acting weird, talking in riddles, then we started talking about our families... things went downhill pretty fast. I looked at him more closely and quickly caught on to what our meeting was meant to be really about."

"The trafficking," I supply.

"Yes, basically," he murmurs, looking down at the open files. "I know this must be really painful for you, but there are some questions I need to still ask you about your mother, that can help us catch her killer."

I fiddle with my hands under the table to stop them from shaking and say, "Ask away, I want to be done with this."

. . . .

I WALK OUT OF THE STATION in a daze, not really seeing what's around me. I squeeze my hands into tight fists and walk through the parking lot toward my car. Before I can get there, a wave of nausea hits me, and I bend toward the nearest bush to throw up my lunch. Violent heaves shudder through my body as hot tears slide over my cheeks.

"Oh God," I gasp and rest my hands on my knees, so I don't fall over. My mother is dead. She was murdered. Brutally. In cold blood. She's gone, and I will never see her soft smile ever again. My son will never meet her. I truly have no other family left apart from Henry.

I straighten from my position and quickly wipe my face with my sleeve, just as a distressed voice reaches me, "Jennifer, are you all right?"

It's Robert. He runs in my direction with a bottle of water in hand, then uncaps it and extends it to me with a worried expression on his face. "Here, dear, drink this."

I nod in appreciation and take a small sip, so I don't get sick again. My hand is still trembling slightly, but the initial shock is over for now.

"Rob, is everything all right there?" I hear being called from some distance behind me. It's a voice I thought I would never hear again in my life. I stiffen and involuntarily squeeze the bottle I'm holding, making the water spill onto my palm. Before I can even think about it, I turn on my heel and there he is.

"Brody?" I mutter disbelievingly and swipe at my eyes, thinking I'm so wrecked that I'm starting to hallucinate.

The man who's been haunting my dreams for the last three years freezes in place when his eyes jump from Robert to my face, and I see the confusion on his face before it gets whipped away and cold indifference sets in its place as he walks toward us.

His jaw is clenched when he says to Robert, "Sorry, I didn't take your calls, man. I was on a job. You didn't have to send your guys to get me. So, I hope it's important."

Brody glances toward me and then gives the detective a meaningful stare, like he's angry at the man that I'm here. That's not a reaction I would anticipate from him in a million years at seeing me again, and I try not to let it show on my face, but damn does that add salt to the wound in my already bleeding heart.

I open my mouth to address him but am cut off by Robert. "It is important. It's about Wallace."

I flinch a little in surprise when Brody hisses, "What the fuck? You know I'm done with this shit. I told you..."

"We found Marissa Wallace. She's been murdered," Robert says bluntly, but his eyes are tormented. I grimace and involuntarily squeeze the bottle again, which reminds me that I'm still holding it. Brody's shocked gaze slams into me, regret written all over his face.

I clear my throat and turn to Robert. "Thanks for the water... I need to get home now. I'll... let you two get back to it."

Not waiting for a response, I get in my beat-up car and drive away.

· · · ·

121

AFTER I COME BACK FROM the station, I feel completely drained and detached from reality, so I don't even as much as frown at Rita's yapping about me being late and talking about what a shitty mom I am. I ignore her and put the electric kettle on to heat some water.

Then I just pluck my fussing son out of her arms wordlessly and carry him into the bathroom. I give him a rubber duck to distract him while I pour some cold water into the bathtub to mix it with the hot water from the kettle. After I make sure the temperature is right, I give him a quick bath.

My movements are sluggish and uncertain, and I blink slowly at my soapy hands. I'm so out of it, that I move completely on autopilot, not really comprehending what's happening around me. Caring for my child is the only instinct breaking through the ripping feeling of despair.

While I am drying Henry with a towel, I notice moisture dropping onto his little head and look up in wonderment. Why is the ceiling leaking? I muse in my mind, only to realize that this whole time, fat streams of sad tears were running down my face.

"What the fuck is the matter with you?" Rita's voice registers in my mind, and it's like someone unmuted the entire world because I suddenly hear my son's loud cries.

"Mamma, mamma, cry! No cry! Mommy!" His face is twisted in distress as he looks up at me, wiggling his arms trying to reach my face.

"Shit," I mutter under my breath and swipe the wetness from my face. I smile and take Henry into my arms. "Mommy doesn't cry, you see? It's just water."

"Is sad?" my son asks with a pout and puts his small palm on my face.

"I'm a little sad. But I'm not crying, you see?" I ask cheerfully and point to my blotchy face.

Fortunately, my two-year-old doesn't need that much convincing and starts babbling happily about his day with grandma. Or at least that's what I think he talks about because many times I don't understand a word from his mouth.

I take him into his room to dress him, feeling Rita's presence hot on my heels, the smell of cigarette smoke wafting around her like a smelly cloud.

"Are you on something? You're acting weird," she says angrily and tries to go around me to take a hold of Henry.

I stop her with my arm and whisper pleadingly, "Please just leave him, I need my son right now. I need to take care of him."

Whatever she sees in my eyes must convince her it's okay to leave me around a child because she backs away after giving her grandson a pat on the head with her wrinkled hand. My boy, oblivious to everything around him, continues with his mindless babbling, while I put on some warmer pajamas on his wiggling chubby body. Then I give him a tickle, and his unrestricted giggles feel like a warm balm on my painted heart.

I carry him to my bed and put on a cartoon on the small TV set right next to my bed. It immediately catches his attention, and I get the time to study his perfect little face.

When Henry's body relaxes and his rhythmic breaths get deeper, I snuggle into him and sniff his soft locks of hair, thinking about everything that I lost.

CHAPTER VIII

I t's been two days since my world was turned upside down again, and I spent yesterday lying in bed and watching Henry play with his toys on the carpet. To my surprise, Rita went out to deal with the unpaid bill. Of course she had to take the money out of my purse to do that, but still, I was grateful when the heating started working again. Right away, I took a long hot shower, just to feel human again.

Today I had to get back to work because even though all I wanted to do was curl into a ball and cry for months, I couldn't exactly do that with all the bills piling up. Life and commitments wait for no one, even the grieving ones.

After the first hours of busting about the diner, I know I probably don't exhort enough enthusiasm while serving my customers. Judging by the tips alone, they're not buying my fake smile today. I just can't find the strength in me anymore to fake it. I used to be so good at that.

There's a tap on my shoulder as I'm stacking dirty dishes from a table. The other waitress, Mary, motions with her thumb toward a table in the back of the diner.

"This one over there asked for you," she murmurs.

Without looking to where she pointed, I refocus on my task and in a monotone voice respond, "That's your section for today."

Mary snorts. "Yeah, tell that guy. He was pretty adamant about it. Oh, he said his name's Damon."

I almost drop the dishes I'm carrying, and then whip my head to the side to see for myself.

"Great," I mutter and eye a stiff-looking Brody from across the room. "Thanks, I'll take care of it."

She nods and moves away to take the next order from a new customer.

I go to dispose of the stack of dirty plates, and then nervously try to smooth my hair, before taking a deep breath and marching over to the table.

"Welcome to Gary's, what can I get for you?" I chirp at Brody, squeezing the hell out of the notepad in my hand.

"I'm not here for the food," he states and blinks slowly. "Can we talk?"

Ignoring his question, I respond with, "Oh, I'm sorry, sir, but this is a diner. If you're not going to order anything, I'm going to have to ask you to leave, please."

"Fine. Coffee, then," he says, his nostrils flaring as he stares me down.

"Sure. Anything else?" I smile at him politely, my cheeks hurting from the exaggerated muscle use.

He takes a breath and licks his lips. "Yeah. You could cut the shit, Jen, and sit the fuck down, so we can talk."

I look behind me to see if anyone is paying attention to us and then answer in a lower voice, "I'm at work. I can't just sit around with random men and chatter whenever I want to."

"Random men? That's what I am now?" he questions with a hard expression on his face.

I sigh and scratch behind my ear, checking the surroundings once again. "You seemed as if you'd rather pretend not to know me in front of the station, so I was trying to respect it. Whatever it is that you want to talk about, I can't right now."

"Fine. What time do you finish?" he demands and starts to get up from his seat.

"Five, but..." I frown when he drops twenty dollars on the table.

Already walking past me, he takes hold of my wrist and squeezes it briefly once before letting go with a silent, "I'll see you then. Thanks for the coffee."

"I didn't bring you any..." I say, but he's already walking out the door. "What the hell?" I whisper and collect the money he left with a shake of my head.

· · · ·

I WALK OUT OF THE DINER tired and overwhelmed. I had to keep my emotions in check the whole day, and the visit from Brody at my workplace didn't help.

"I'm here, what is it that you want to talk about?" I ask without meeting his gaze and tap my foot impatiently after I lean on his car, that's been parked close to the entrance for the last hour.

He clears his throat. "I'm sorry about how I acted the day before," Brody says slowly, and I glance at him before looking to the side again.

"That's fine. We don't know each other anymore. You don't owe me an explanation," I say with a raised chin and grab my keys out of my pocket. "If that's all..."

"No, I..." He curses under his breath. "Could you at least look at me?"

Tilting my head slowly, I look at his tortured face and gulp.

Brody takes a step closer and says, "Look, I didn't anticipate ever seeing you again. That part of my life was closed. Then I saw you, and it all hit me like a ton of bricks."

"Sorry for the inconvenience..." I state and step away, ready to flee.

Brody growls in his throat and throws his hands up in exasperation, before chuckling. His laugh is what freezes me in place.

I turn to him and give him the stink eye. "What's funny?"

Brody shakes his head, and smirks. "It's just good to see that some things don't change. You're still as frustrating as I remember."

"Thanks," I say sarcastically.

"So, as I was saying..." He throws me a look, daring me to interrupt him again. "I'm sorry for how I reacted. It's been three years and I honestly didn't think you'd be living right under my nose in Madison. Things that happened in Bell Ridge back then, with your father... it messed me up for a long time. I guess I'm still a little salty about it. Seeing you just brought all that back, but then..." He lifts a hand, stopping me from interjecting. "I knew I was wrong for associating you with all that shit that happened in the past. You were the victim. Again, I'm sorry, Jen."

"Oh." I bite my lip, not knowing how to react to his apology. It's been a long time since anyone acknowledged, and more importantly regretted, treating me badly. "I mean, it's cool. We're cool." I gesture between us with a hand. "I didn't think I would see you again, too, least of all places at the police station."

Brody winces. "Yeah, I'm so sorry about your mom, sweetheart."

"Thank you. I still can't believe this is real," I say in a frail voice. "They think my father did it. Do you believe he's capable of doing that?"

Brody's face hardens before he states, "I have no doubt about it."

I hum in my throat and lick my lips. "I still think that they will call me back to say there's been a mistake. That it was someone else's body. But in my heart, I know it's her. He killed my mom..." I swipe at the tear that escapes my eye.

When I look at his sad face, I feel my own regret and pain squeeze me by the heart. Before the dam on my feelings breaks right here in the parking lot, and I have a meltdown, I quickly throw, "I have to go," and whirl around.

Brody calls after me, but I don't look back as I power walk to my car. Then I get out of here.

• • • •

"ARE YOU GOING BACK to the old habits, and stalking me again?" I say teasingly to Brody the next day, as I lean on his car, leaving a few feet of space between us.

I'm still shattered by my mother's death, and not completely accepting the reality, but today has been a little better. Robert called to inform me, that in accordance with my wishes, my mother's body was cremated, and her ashes were buried in a collective grave at Madison Cemetery. I'm not sure why it was so important to me, but the thought of my mom finally being able to rest in peace brought me immense relief.

"Checking on you is not the same as stalking." Brody crosses his arms and throws me a look.

I smile coyly at him. "Just admit already that you're still obsessed with me."

Brody snorts but looks to the side without answering for a second, then looks back at me with a more serious expression as he changes the subject. "How are you holding up?"

I take a breath and rub my arms when a shiver runs through me. "I've been better. Honestly, I'm not sure how I feel. In a way, I lost my mom a long time ago. I'm torn about the whole thing. In one moment, I feel sad and heartbroken, and betrayed and hateful a second later. I feel like I should only hate my father. But if I'm honest, sometimes I hate both of them equally," I say shamefully, and concentrate on Brody's sad eyes as he listens to me studiously. "I obviously had my issues with Mom, she wasn't perfect and she's hurt me. You know all that. I guess somewhere in the back of my head, I thought there will come a time when she comes begging for my forgiveness, it's messed up..."

Brody lifts his hand to squeeze my shoulder in support, and then drops it when I look down.

He clears his throat and says, "I don't know if this will be any consolation, but I worked with Robert before and he is a great detective. If anyone can catch your bastard father, it's him. And you can tell that he's fully committed to the case."

"Yeah, maybe... Aren't you working on the case too?" I ask and frown when Brody shakes his head with an uncomfortable expression on his face.

"No, uh." He scratches his head. "I'm not working for the FBI anymore. Actually, that's one of the things I wanted to talk about. I think there are still some facts that you need to know. I mean... about what happened back then. Why I wasn't there..."

"Oh, I'm not sure..." I start, backing away slightly.

Brody lifts his hands in a pleading gesture. "Please, Jen. We could go get something to eat and if I could just explain..."

"You don't have to explain anything," I reply stubbornly.

He straightens from the car and throws angrily, "But I need to, Jen! I can't fucking go on living like this. The thought that I couldn't be there for you still kills me. The idea of you believing that I abandoned you or something, rips me apart every goddamn day!"

I'm so taken aback by this sudden display of emotion on Brody's part that I don't even take notice of him getting closer. I look up at him in question, when he's suddenly right in front of me.

"Just one meal. We talk. I tell you everything that went down. And if you decide you're done with me, then we'll be done. That's all I'm asking, Jen."

"I can't," I say regretfully, and when Brody opens his mouth to speak, I rush to reassure him. "Not because I don't want to, okay? I just... I need to get back home," I step around him, to leave more space between us, and breathe. "Maybe some other time, alright?"

I leave him there looking hurt and confused, but I truly can't deal with this now. I march toward my car, and praise the old junk when it starts on the first try.

• • • •

THE NEXT DAY, IT'S almost the end of my shift when Gary comes to me and glances through the window. "Just put the guy out of his misery already," he says jokingly, and I glance up at him from the table I'm cleaning.

"The man who's been coming to see you." He tilts his head to the side, and I look in that direction. My eyebrows lift in surprise when I notice Brody leaning by his car yet again.

"Whatever he did, either forgive him or cut him loose completely, girly. He looks like the stubborn type, so just deal with it. One way or the other." Then he turns and walks away, leaving me there gazing at Brody's stiff silhouette as he glares across the parking lot, looking miserable.

One way or the other. Fine.

"Three days in a row. I have to admit that you're persistent," I say and step into my usual spot next to Brody. "As always, I have to disappoint you and tell you that I won't be going anywhere with you today." I lift my finger to press it to Brody's mouth, keeping in the smile that threatens to break on my face when I see the surprised lift of his eyebrows. "Shush, let me finish."

Brody hums in his throat and I remove the finger. "I won't be coming anywhere with you today. But since you're so hell-bent on stalking me, I will agree to have dinner with you on my day off..."

A slow smile spreads on Brody's handsome face. "Wow, that was easy."

"But there's a catch," I announce and make a dramatic pause.

"What is it?" Brody frowns.

"I won't be coming alone," I state seriously and bite my lip.

I'm not ashamed of my son, but people tend to react weirdly when they realize I'm a young single mother, so I'm a little anxious to drop the news on Brody. I'm sure he would never even put the old Jenny and a baby in one sentence before.

Brody deflates slightly and mutters, "Oh. I didn't think you were seeing anyone."

"I'm not. But there is a man in my life. Rather permanently," I smirk when Brody automatically glances down at my hand, probably in search of a ring.

When he focuses back on my face, he wears the most confused expression. There's also something dark in his eyes, and it's the first time I'm seeing it.

Before I put him out of his misery, I decide to torture him, for the old times' sake, seeing that he truly seems bothered by the thought of me getting hitched.

"His name is Henry, and he's the reason I'm always rushing to get back home. I can't go long without him. After a long day of work, I just miss him something fierce, you know?"

Brody's jaw clenches, and he grunts, before I continue with an oblivious, dreamy smile. "Things have been so much easier with him since he learned how to use the potty, let me tell you..."

His head snaps back in shock. "The... What?"

This time, I can't hold in the laughter for a second longer. I bend over and giggle uncontrollably, with a new fit hitting me each time I come up for air and see Brody looking at me like he's unable to decide if he should run or call an ambulance.

"The look... on your... face." I wheeze and wipe the tears from my eyes. "Oh my god, that was the first time I laughed like that in a long time. Thanks, Handsome."

"Uh... I'm so confused right now," he says uncertainly and steps from foot to foot.

"I'm so sorry, it's actually the first time I have to tell someone the news, and I guess I've been a little nervous to see how you'll react." I smile and roll my eyes. "I have a son, Brody."

He tilts his head to the side and asks slowly, "You have a kid?"

"Yup," I chirp. "His name is Henry. He just turned two," I say proudly and use the fact that Brody is immobilized with the bomb I dropped on him to take out my phone to show him pictures of my baby.

He looks down in wonderment at the photo, and I swipe to show him one of the two of us together. Brody's face gentles when he says, "He looks just like you."

"I know. Isn't that a blessing?" I joke and take the phone back. "So as you can see, if I'm going anywhere, this fine little gentleman will have to tag along."

"That's fine." Brody chuckles. Then his smile dies down when he seems to think over something.

"Spill," I demand.

"Umm, I don't mean to pry, but what about the kid's father?" he asks without meeting my gaze completely.

I wave my hand dismissively. "He's out of the picture."

Brody grimaces. "So you've been on your own? Jen, you're so..."

"Young?" I interject irritably. "I know, the doctor who delivered him kept saying it, but I still couldn't just push him back in where he came from."

"What the fuck?" Brody slaps a hand to his face, then throws me an incredulous look. "I meant to say you're so brave, Jen. Brave. Jesus Christ."

"Oh." I frown. "Then, I guess, I should say thanks."

Brody blows a breath. "Okay, so since we've got this settled. When is your next day off work?"

"This Sunday," I answer.

"Oh. I promised my aunt that I'll stop by on Sunday. She's been on my ass constantly lately about not dropping by often enough."

"That's fine, we can meet some other time then..." I say and look down when my phone starts ringing. "Shit, it's Rita. I have to go," I say apologetically.

"No. Wait." Brody throws my way when I start to back away. "How about you go with me to the shelter? Ruth would be ecstatic to see you."

"I don't know." I scratch behind my ear, still walking backwards to my car.

"Do you remember where it is?" Brody asks and opens the door to his car.

I nod from across the parking lot, and before I even open my mouth to decline the invitation, Brody smiles and exclaims, "Great! See you and the little guy, Sunday at six." Then he slams the door after him and quickly peels away, leaving a cloud of dust in his wake.

I'm blinking after the disappearing tail lights, when my phone pings once again with a message from Rita. I groan and get in, cursing myself already for not being firm enough about the invitation.

When I turn on the key in the ignition, the car coughs and nothing happens.

"No. Please don't give up on me," I beg it.

I try again and mutter, "Please, you can do this. You can do this." When the engine starts, I cheer with a bounce and put the car in gear.

Then I whisper under my breath, "Yes, you can do this."

CHAPTER IX

"Where are you going?" Rita wobbles into my room with Henry in her arms, before she eyes me as I try on the only presentable dress I own at the moment.

"I'm meeting with some friends," I respond noncommittally, and glance at my reflection in the mirror. As usual, I'm not wearing any makeup, but I did try to arrange my hair into something different from the tangled knot on the top of my head. I braided it to the side, leaving a few loose curly strands to frame my face. It's been awhile since I wore anything besides sweats or my waitress uniform, so it instantly makes me feel more confident about going out.

"Friends?" The older woman scoffs and comes closer to tug on the hem of my dress, which ends at mid-thigh. "Dressed like this? You better not fuck around behind my son's back."

Giving her a side look, I smack my lips irritably and say, "Don't make it seem like I'm going naked. I went to job interviews in it, and you said I looked presentable back then. And not that's any of your business, but as I said, I'm going to hang out with some friends, not to fuck around."

"You should've told me before, that I'm going to be stuck here with the little one," Rita grumbles but pats Henry on the head.

"You're not. He's going with me," I turn to her fully and retrieve Henry, who giggles happily when I tickle his feet before I place him on my hip, and move to retreat my bag with all the baby stuff from the nightstand.

Right before I exit my bedroom, I pause next to a glaring Rita and give her my serious face. "Before I go, let's make one thing clear. I am grateful for you letting us stay here, but know that this doesn't earn you the right to comment on my private life. I'm not going on a date or whatever it is you're thinking. But if I were, it shouldn't be a problem. I'm done with your son, Rita. Ricky had his chance and he blew it."

"Ricky is a good boy. If you'd finally answered his calls, and let him explain. He made some mistakes. That's it." She raises her chin at her grandson. "And he's still Henry's father. You shouldn't keep his son away from him."

"I have nothing to say to him, so you can tell him to stop calling. And while you're at it, tell him that doing the bare minimum before ending up in a prison doesn't make someone a father. And if Ricky didn't want to be kept away from his son, maybe he should've thought of that before he and his idiotic friends decided to steal a goddamn car." I pin her with an icy stare and then look down at Henry. "We're going on a trip! Say bye to grandma."

My son smiles and waves excitedly at Rita, completely oblivious to the daggers the woman still shoots at me, and exclaims, "Byeee, nannnyyy!"

"Yeah, bye nanny," I sing cheerfully with a wink and exit the room.

• • • •

SINCE PUTTING AN OVEREXCITED two-year-old into a car seat always proves to be a challenge, it's not surprising that I'm running late. My palms sweat as I park in front of the shelter. I take a deep breath to calm myself as I eye the building that I escaped from three years ago. Now it feels like it happened in another lifetime, so much has happened since that day.

When Henry starts kicking the passenger seat to express his impatience, I snap out of it and exit the vehicle before letting him out and retrieving the big bag from the passenger seat. From the corner of my eye, I can see my son is ready to take off and turn quickly to get a hold of him, only to witness him running straight into a pair of jean-clad legs.

Brody catches him right before he can bounce off to the ground with a chuckle. "Whoa, hey there, buddy. Where are you off to? Aren't you gonna wait for your mommy?"

Surprised by the giant in front of him, Henry grabs onto his leg and tilts his head all the way back, before putting his hand to his mouth in awe.

"Toy..." Henry mutters right before I lift him from the ground.

"You mean Thor, baby, not Toy. And this is my friend Brody. Say hi." Henry extends his hand shyly toward the man, and then hides his head in my neck.

I peer at Brody, who looks at us with a soft expression and laugh awkwardly. "Sorry, I've just introduced him to some superheroes. I guess, he thinks he just met a celebrity."

"That's cool. Being called Thor is so much better than the Hulk." He winks at me, and I smirk. "Let me take this..."

"Oh, no, that's fine..." I mutter as Brody takes the heavy bag off my shoulder, and of course, it falls on deaf ears because he already turns toward the entrance and waves us in.

"Come on, Ruth has been so thrilled to hear that you're coming, she's been all over the place."

139

Just as he says this, the woman herself steps in the doorway and almost rams into Brody in her haste to get to me with her arms wide open.

"Jenny! I'm so happy to see you!" Aunt Ruth embraces me, squishing Henry between our bodies. Then she moves back to look at the toddler. "Oh my god, aren't you the cutest? Come to your auntie, I swear I will spoil you rotten, you little heartbreaker."

I'm surprised when Henry willingly goes into Ruth's arms, looking enchanted with her puffy white hair.

"Let me take a look at you." The woman surveys me from head to toe and shakes her head in disapproval. "My, you're way too skinny. We'll need to feed you right away." Her hand moves to my face with a sincere smile. "But you did grow to be even more beautiful. No wonder the boy lost his head," she says only for me to hear, then calls over her shoulder, "Damon, doesn't Jenny look beautiful?"

I feel my face heat immediately and look toward him, thinking that he'll laugh it off, but I'm frozen in place when our eyes meet, and I don't see any humor in his stare.

He looks at me from head to toe, and then replies in a raspy voice, "She sure does, Aunt Ruth."

I gulp and contain the need to fan my face, which probably is tomato red right now. Shit, this can't be happening to me. I thought I was over my teenage crush on the man, and now here he is saying shit like that, and I'm back to being seventeen.

Shifting my weight from foot to foot, I clear my throat and look back at Ruth, who looks between her nephew and me with a cunning smile.

"Thank you for having me, Ruth. I'm sorry that I never came to say thank you for... After..." I rub my hands together, trying to find the words to express my gratitude, but also my regret of never coming back to do just that.

I can't even put anything together because Ruth is already shaking her head. "That's all in the past, dear. You're here now, and I couldn't be happier to see that you've made it whole. That's all I've been praying for. For you to survive. The same goes for my boy."

Before I get to question her about what she means by that, she whirls around with Henry and gets inside.

I look back at Brody questioningly, but he only waves his hand and says, "After you."

As soon as I'm inside, the familiar scents of home-cooked meals and female chatter hit me, and my eyes water involuntarily when the pleasant memories emerge from the parts of my mind I kept behind a mental wall. I've only been here for a week years ago, and it wasn't for holidays, but it was still special to me. A warm place with friendly faces and Aunt Ruth as this sort-of motherly figure to help navigate through my days. I didn't even realize how much I missed it before coming back here.

"Come on in. When I told Amelia that you'll be coming, she was over the moon. She's been on a cleaning spree. I told her she shouldn't scrub toilets in her state, but the woman is so stubborn..."

"So, Amelia is still here?" I question excitedly, extending my hand for Henry to grab onto, when Ruth puts him on the ground. Of course, right now, I seem to be invisible because he grabs onto her skirt and patters with his small feet to keep up with her step.

"Oh yes, but they aren't living here anymore. Amelia is still the cook, thank God, and the girls often visit, but it's just not the same as having them all here..."

I follow the older woman and look around at the few changes and adjustments in the place. I'm delighted to see that the shelter seems to be doing better these days.

Before we reach the kitchen and dining room, Ruth stops and turns to her nephew. "Damon, be a sweetheart and go to the upstairs bathroom to check on that leak under the faucet."

Brody's eyebrows lift in question, but the woman continues with a smarmy smile, "You know where to find the tools. The dinner is not ready yet anyway."

"Sure," he grunts and retreats into one of the corridors.

I look at his retreating form and then back at Ruth when she says, "That will give him some time to cool down, and give us the time to catch up."

"Why does he need to cool down? Did I do something?" I ask worriedly.

Ruth smirks and looks down at Henry. "Your momma is totally oblivious, ain't she?"

When the kid nods his head, not even understanding what he is agreeing to, she laughs under her breath, and then takes in my confused expression. "You're not ready to see it, I get it. Just don't give him false hope, if it's not possible."

"I don't..." I start and jump away when the door to the kitchen bangs open.

"How much longer will you keep me waiting? I thought I heard..." Amelia notices me standing next to Ruth and drops the washcloth she was holding. "Oh! I can't believe it!"

She comes closer and embraces me in an awkward hug. It's awkward because I'm staring at her in bewilderment, stiff as a board. Three years ago, Amelia would've freaked out at such an intimate contact, but now she is the one initiating it.

Finally, I pat her gently on the back, and she moves away to look up at me. At my height I tower over most women, so it's nothing new, but Amelia looks almost like a little fairy next to me. She smiles at me softly and then without a warning bursts out crying. I jump in shock and look to Ruth for help, but she only rolls her eyes.

"Hormones," the woman mumbles with a pout, but her eyes are smiling.

"Hormones?" I parrot and then widen my eyes when I look down and notice the baby bump on Amelia, who continues to lament dramatically.

"Come on, Amelia. You're spooking the little one." Ruth motions to Henry, who hides behind her to observe the scene. His mouth starts wobbling like he's on a verge of joining the pregnant woman in the cry fest.

"Henry, everything is fine," I tell him over Amelia's head.

When I say that, she turns to see who I'm talking to and exclaims, "Oh! Is this your little man? Jenny! He's adorable."

"That's my son, Henry," I say proudly and smile at him, when I see his curiosity win, as he removes himself from Ruth's dress and walks toward the crying stranger.

"No cry," he says to her, before patting her on the leg. He turns to me and raises his arms, indicating that I take him, and I do just that.

"He's not really used to meeting new people. I think he might be overwhelmed," I mutter when Henry tries to hide his head into my neck again.

"So precious," Amelia muses, before swiping at her tears. "Please excuse my waterworks. It's been happening constantly."

I laugh at that, and trail after both women when they start leading us to the kitchen. "I can relate. I've been a crying, moody bitch throughout the whole pregnancy."

Amelia giggles as she pushes me to sit in one of the chairs, with Henry placed in my lap. "Yeah, I feel for my fiancé. I'm surprised he hadn't run for the hills yet."

"So, who's the lucky guy?" I ask giddily.

"His name is Mark," Amelia answers dreamily. "About a year ago, Sammy started to complain about stomach aches. So, we went to see a pediatrician. Turned out she had appendicitis."

"Shit, I'm sorry. Is she okay?"

Amelia waves her hand dismissively before grabbing a cookie from a plate and giving it to Henry. "She's fine. Both she and Silvia are watching TV upstairs as we speak. Anyway, Mark was the surgeon operating on my girl. I was so grateful and wanted to thank him for his good work, so I asked him out for lunch. He said yes, and the rest is history, as they say."

"Wow," I whisper and lean my head on my hand. "That's wonderful, Amelia. I'm so happy for you. How far along are you?"

"Six months," she says proudly and rubs her small bump.

"No way! This is six months?" I point at her stomach. "I looked like a freakin' barrow at six months with this little guy. So unfair," I mutter playfully.

"I'm sure you're exaggerating." Amelia laughs, then takes the seat opposite me. "Since we have some time before the roast is ready, why don't you tell us what you've been up to after you jumped out of that window."

"Don't remind me that I did that," I wince and grumpily add, "My back has never been the same."

Amelia grins. "I bet. But it was pretty badass."

"Badass..." Ruth scoffs and throws a stink eye her way as she moves around the kitchen. "I almost had a heart attack when you told me she jumped out. That was stupid. I'm glad you didn't break anything, Jenny."

"Don't worry, Ruth. I'm stronger than I look." I wink at her.

"That you are." I whirl around at the deep male voice coming from the doorway.

"Are you done, boy?" the older woman asks Brody as she dries her hands with a towel.

"I stopped the leak upstairs, but also noticed some loose tiles between the shower stalls and one of the drains is clogged. I'll come by some other day after work to fix it." He takes a seat next to us, and without hesitation gives his hand to Henry to play with when he wiggles his little chocolate cookie-smudged fingers. "So what did I miss?"

"Jenny was just about to tell the tale about her big escape," Amelia informs him.

Three pairs of eyes focus on me, and I stiffen, my arms tightening around Henry. "Oh, I...I don't..." I stumble over my words and then take a deep breath to calm myself. "What do you want to know?"

• • • •

"ANYWAY, IS LUCY STILL around?" I ask with hope in my voice, as I sit back in one of the couches in the common room.

After dinner, we moved here from the kitchen so that Henry could play with the shelter kids in the set-out playpen full of toys. I took a spot from which I had a direct view of my kid and was surprised when Brody sat down right next to me, with our arms rubbing against each other.

"Lucy? Oh, she was here for a while. She got a job in Miami last year and decided to move there. Figured it's far enough to start a new life," Ruth answers with a satisfied grin.

"Really? Wow, good for her," I smile, trying to hide my disappointment. I don't know why I thought she'd maybe still be here. It's been three years. Of course, she had to move on from the shelter.

"Lucy left her contact in here if we wanted to reach her. I'm sure she'd be happy to hear from you," Amelia reads my expression and answers kindly.

I smile back at her, but then freeze when Brody asks in a hard voice, "So, why didn't you come back to the shelter after some time? I gathered that you liked it here. If you knew it's safe to come back, and you had to know it at some point if you still stayed in Madison, then why stay away?"

"Oh, I think we'll let you two talk in private now. Let's go, Amelia." Ruth gets up, looking uncomfortable, and pulls up Amelia with her.

146

"Yes. It's time for me and the girls anyway," the pregnant woman says and gives me a hug. "It was wonderful to see you, Jenny. I'm glad you're okay."

"I hope we can catch up some time, maybe you can come by with the girls to the diner after my shift or something," I offer helpfully.

"I would love to! Give me your number and I'll text you."

We exchange phone numbers, and after saying goodbyes, both women leave with encouraging smiles.

I sit back down next to Brody, who's watching Henry play with a toy car, totally ignorant of people walking past him.

"I didn't want to live," I break the silence and can see Brody's head turn toward me, but I don't look at him, still concentrating on my son.

"I was tired of running, of my life, I just didn't care anymore. I didn't care to ever come back. I was just done." I lick my dry lips and rub my arms, feeling uncharacteristically cold. "When I met Ricky, I just let things happen, you know? He offered me a good time, booze, drugs, and even bought me some stuff. I didn't ask questions, I didn't react to anything. I was numb. I just wanted to cease to exist."

"Sweetheart, that's..." Brody grunts sorrowfully and reaches for my hand. "I'm sorry."

"If it wasn't for him..." I nod toward Henry. "I wouldn't be here. That I'm sure of. Because I never tried to kill myself, per se. But I didn't hang onto life either. Until I found out I was pregnant a few months after running away. And suddenly, it's like this fog was cleared from my brain. I was given a purpose for the first time in my life. A reason to live. To care for myself."

Brody hums in his throat and then asks, "What about that Ricky guy you've mentioned? You said Henry's father is out of the picture before."

"Yeah..." I sigh and focus on Brody's intense eyes. "He wasn't the greatest, but the fact that he didn't beat me or hurt me was a big step-up in my mind at the time. I was his girl, and I was happy with all the drugs he could provide. It was simple. But then I was knocked up."

"Let me guess. Ricky wasn't a fan of the idea of becoming a father..." Brody grouses disapprovingly.

"Understatement." I snort and roll my eyes. "For me, the party was over, and I started to make demands. Ricky was there for me sometimes... but mostly I was just a pregnant roommate in a house full of mayhem. After I gave birth, things turned for the worse, but at least I still had a roof over my head and food in my belly. Then, when Henry was just maybe a month, Ricky started to fuck around with someone else."

"You guys broke up?" Brody questions, and starts to swipe his thumb against my palm, reminding me that my hand is still in his grasp. When did we move on to holding hands? Does it mean something, or is this just a friendly show of support on his part? Am I just reading too much into it?

"Jen?" Brody prompts, and I snap my eyes to his.

"What? Oh. Umm, we separated, but not really. Henry and I still lived with Ricky and his friends for a while," I mutter distractedly.

"So where is he?"

I scratch my neck irritably before I answer. "Idiot got himself into trouble. From what I found out later, his moronic friends decided to make some fast money. Of course, they were all too stupid to pull anything off, and instead were fast thrown into jail. Auto theft."

Brody's eyebrows lift, but he doesn't comment, so I continue with my story. "Anyway. I couldn't stay at that house anymore. So, I decided to stop being a chicken shit, and finally solve all that shit from my past. I packed our stuff, and drove with Henry back to Bell Ridge."

"Wait. You came back there?" Brody sits straighter and squeezes my hand with a disturbed expression on his face.

I wave my free hand with a pout, remembering that awful day. "Waste of time, but at least the cop I spoke to shed some light on my situation. Although, he was a dick."

"Which cop?" Brody asks with a frown, looking back at Henry when he starts making noise.

"I don't know... Davis? Dines?"

"Diaz?" Brody supplies and I snap my fingers.

"Yes! That's the one." I smack my lips, when I recollect my encounter with the police officer. "He told me there were no charges against me anymore, and that my parents were gone. That you're gone. That Claire's gone. Asshole just about told me to get the fuck out and to never come back because all I bring is trouble," I laugh derisively, when I see the sneering face in my mind. "And when he saw Henry? God, I thought he was going to shit a brick. Weird man."

I look back at Brody when he takes his hand away from mine and leans forward to rest his elbows on his knees with a sour expression.

"What?" I glance at my son to see if he's still preoccupied and then turn my body fully toward Brody, to squeeze his arm. "Brody, what is it?"

He rakes his hand through his hair and exhales. "A lot happened back then. I guess you've already heard about the fire at the warehouse, and your father being on the run after that."

"Robert mentioned something," I reply in a low voice, curious where this is going.

"I was there," Brody admits quietly and finally faces me again. "In that warehouse. With your father," he clarifies when I cast him a confused look.

"I fucked up, Jen. With so many things. I put you in danger, myself, the whole investigation, hell, even Diaz almost died because of me."

"But you did expose the sheriff, right?" I question.

"That fucking fire did start off a sequence of events that eventually led to issuing an arrest warrant. But I will never take credit for that. And it's not like we got the guy. He's still out there. He was free to..." He stops with regret written on his face, but we both know what he was about to say. My father was still free to kill my mother, and he's still free to kill someone else.

Brody takes a breath and sits back to get a hold of my hand again. "I'm sorry, I wasn't there. I know that's not what you want to hear, but I need to say my piece."

I nod my head for him to go on, and put my free hand on top of our clasped palms.

"I'm not making excuses for myself. But I got hurt pretty badly in the fire, so the first weeks after that, I wasn't even a part of the manhunt. The burns on my body were pretty severe. I had to undergo a few skin transplants and surgeries. The pain was so severe at times, I actually considered ending it all..." he says reluctantly, and I retrieve my hand to cover my mouth as I gasp. "Anyway, when I was ready to get back on my feet, the whole population of Bell Ridge was already like an enraged swarm of bees. Turned out, your father wouldn't leave without sowing even more chaos into my world. An anonymous letter was delivered to the station, containing photographs of each of our meetings. Some of them looked... suggestive, when you were joking around, and things like that." Brody glances away, looking abashed. "On top of everything that happened, I was a suspect now for soliciting a minor."

"You're fucking joking," I say, my eyes wide with disbelief. "They actually thought that because of some stupid pictures?"

He clears his throat and nods. "Of course, the charges were dropped eventually due to lack of evidence. But I was mostly done in Bell Ridge. Done in the law enforcement too."

"Jesus Christ," I whisper and rub at my chest.

"I think it could explain Diaz's reaction to you, and to the kid," Brody tilts his head toward Henry, who looks ready to drop at any second. "Probably thought he was mine or something."

I stand up and take the tired, fussing toddler into my arms, surprised when Brody indicates to pass him over. Henry willingly crawls onto his lap and squishes his face against the giant man's torso before he's dead asleep within seconds.

Brody looks down at the sleeping baby, with a soft smile, and says in a lower voice, "I wouldn't complain if he were mine." My heart skips a beat, and I hold my breath when he peers at me. "But it just shows how narrow-minded people are. I would never do that with you."

I swear I hear a balloon pop somewhere in my brain.

I look away with a snort and try to cover my hurt at hearing that last sentence with a joking tone, "Jeez, Brody. I know I'm far from Miss Universe, but you didn't have to say it like that. I know I'm way out of your league."

"What?" Brody asks incredulously, his head swinging back. He then seems to get what he said and shakes his head, before rearranging sleeping Henry, so he can turn to look directly at me. "That came out wrong. What I meant was that I would never use you like that. I wanted to help you. To think that they assumed I used you at your most fragile and then left you with a baby to fend for yourself is fucking outlandish, Jen. Did I like you? Yes, obviously. Was I into you? Of course, you're beautiful. It was hard for me to..." He stops when he realizes what he just said and grimaces.

I can feel the deflated balloon of hope rising again in my mind. For the life of me, I can't stop the smile that comes to my face. I quickly wipe it off and clear my throat. "I think it's getting pretty late. I need to get the little one to bed, and I have work in the morning."

Brody glances at his watch and mutters, "Yeah, me too."

"So, what is it that you do now, if you're done with the police stuff?" I inquire as we descend the stairs together, Henry sleeping soundly in Brody's arms.

"Construction. My uncle Frank, Ruth's husband, taught me a thing or two in my teenage years, so I decided to put that to good use," he answers with a neutral expression on his face.

"Do you miss working as an agent?" I ask after we say our goodbyes to everyone and exit the building.

Brody hums in his throat before answering, "Not really. I guess it wasn't for me. Maybe I have too much... conscience? I took every case personally, and it proved to be almost deadly for me. Construction feels almost like therapy in a way. It's very soothing to build something and to see the effects of your hard work. I don't know..."

"I'm glad you found something fulfilling after everything," I say and open my car, so Brody can put Henry into his car seat. When the sleeping toddler is strapped in, and Brody straightens from the car, I move closer to him and grab onto his arm.

"I'm sorry you had to go through all of this. Because of my father... because of me," I say quietly.

He reaches his hand toward my face with an intense expression, and just like that last time three years ago, puts the one lock of my hair behind my ear.

"I would go through all of it again, if it meant that you're safe, Jen."

I blink up at him, feeling a wave of sadness hit me all of a sudden. "This isn't a goodbye, right?"

Brody shakes his head, and smiles warmly, before he leans toward me, making my heart gallop. He brushes his lips on my forehead, and mutters, "Not a goodbye, sweetheart. A new beginning." Then he moves back, and says, "Drive safe," before walking away, leaving me by my car with my mouth agape.

What was that?

CHAPTER X

Today is Sunday, which means that, in keeping with our new tradition, we spent the afternoon with Brody and Ruth. As in most cases, we were also joined by Amelia and her fiancé Mark, but with my pregnant friend getting a little closer to giving birth, their stay didn't last very long today.

Aunt Ruth had to take care of a new girl in the middle of dinner, who turned up at the shelter in a not-so-good condition, and so it was just me and Brody left. And of course, Henry, who often acts as a buffer when the atmosphere between us starts to thicken.

To be honest, I'm confused about Brody's behavior lately. Every so often I get signals from him that show me that he is interested in something more than simple friendship, only to act a second later as if nothing had happened.

He's been adjusting his work schedule, to come and see me during my lunch breaks, and we have been regularly seeing each other at the shelter for weeks now. He wouldn't try to spend that much time with me if he weren't interested. Right?

Not to mention all those times, when he makes the small little remarks about how good I look, what a great mother to Henry I am, and how much he admires me. Topping all of that with taking hold of my hand, sporadic forehead kisses, and those subtle, seemingly innocent touches, and I'm a fucking mess around him.

These little gestures, intense glances, and sometimes even shameless flirting on his part drive me crazy. If he feels the same chemistry between us as I do, why doesn't he do something?

After all, it can't be about me having a child. At first, I was afraid that the reason for keeping me at a distance is because of Henry. It soon became apparent that Brody is delighted with my son and is more than happy to spend time with him when we visit.

It cannot be about my past. Nor about the age difference. That part is behind us for some time now, I think.

Then why the fuck doesn't he kiss me already or ask me out, or anything?

I'm thinking all that, when, as usual, Brody walks me to my car, sleeping Henry in his arms. Before we can step outside, he halts me. "Wait, it started raining. Take him for a sec, and I'll go ask Aunt Ruth for an umbrella because I don't see one here."

Without a word, I take my sleeping son from him and watch his fine ass as he retreats from the room. Damn. When the fuck did I get so horny? Lusting after Brody, while my innocent baby sleeps in my arms.

"Get a grip, Jenny," I mutter and whip my head around when I hear steps closer to me than I anticipated.

"Talking to yourself now? You sure have been quiet today. Was the company not meeting your requirements for a good conversation?" Brody teases, umbrella in hand.

"Just a lot on my mind," I say evasively. "Shall we?"

Brody nods, and together we walk into the evening. The rain isn't too heavy, but the dark clouds above us foreshadow an oncoming storm.

"Does he always sleep like this? I swear the kid doesn't even stir," Brody wonders, as he puts Henry into his car seat, and straps him in, his movements practiced now.

"It's a blessing." I smile, and go around to get in.

I turn to say bye, and am surprised by how close to me Brody is standing, umbrella in hand. His face is mostly in the shadow, but I notice the way he eyes my lips.

Just kiss me, I chant in my head, then frown when Brody steps back and clears his throat. "Better get on that road before the storm."

I nod, trying not to show my disappointment. "Bye, Brody. Thank you for the lovely evening," I say grumpily, and his eyebrows lift.

"Was it lovely? It's hard to read that from your tone." He smiles warmly.

I roll my eyes but reciprocate the smile. "Yup. It was. Good night."

"Good night, sweetheart," he says, then closes the door for me, and waits until I start the car.

"Good night, sweetheart," I mimic in a deep voice, as I drive away, then snap my eyes to the rearview mirror to see if Henry is still asleep. "I'm losing my goddamn mind, kiddo. Mommy's got a screw loose somewhere in there." I tap my head, knowing that I'm basically talking to myself.

I shake my head and turn at the intersection, only to groan when my car starts slowing down, before completely shutting down. "Come on, you piece of motherfucking shit," I growl, and try to start it up again.

This whole month this old clunker was giving me a hard time, but at least he coughed and spewed before coming to life when I turned the ignition. Now it's dead silence as the car stands immobilized in the middle of a goddamn road.

"Come on, come on," I say and try again, but nothing happens and I bang on the steering wheel in exasperation.

I look around when I see lights approaching, and make out Brody's car pulling up ahead of us, before he exits the vehicle and runs to us.

"Having car troubles?" he asks when I lower the window.

"Yeah, obviously," I snap like a total bitch, and wince before adding in a softer tone, "Sorry, but the last thing I need right now is a broken car."

"Well, let's take a look then," he states calmly, and motions for me to switch places with him.

"Anyway, what are you doing here?" I ask as I stand in the rain, and watch Brody switching the key in the ignition with a frown. His big body looks ridiculous in the small vehicle.

"I was driving home. Didn't know it wasn't allowed," he mutters and exits. "I'm not a mechanic, but since nothing seems to be working, I would say it's either the battery or the alternator."

"What does that mean?" I question worriedly, ignoring the increasing rain falling on my head.

Brody glances at a car that skirts around us, and then back at me. "Call your insurance company because that car isn't going anywhere today." Then he motions for me to get behind the wheel. "Come on, you can't leave it here like that. Put it in neutral, and I'll push you to the side."

I do as he says, cursing profusely the whole time.

"Do you have the number to the insurance company?" Brody asks, as he bends to look at me through the window again, completely oblivious to the raindrops beating on his head.

"I don't have an insurance," I grumble, looking to the side.

"What?" he asks and moves his head closer to hear me better.

I take a deep breath, and say louder, "I said, I don't have an insurance." I turn my head back and say bitterly, "I'm riding this rusty junkyard on wheels. Do you think I can afford such a thing?"

Brody's eyebrows lift, but he doesn't say anything as he straightens from the window.

I think he's about to leave my rude and whiny ass, so I start lamenting as I bang my head on the steering wheel. "Jesus Christ, what will I do now? I need this fucking car. I live on the other side of the motherfucking town. And even if I get there with Henry today in one piece, how the fuck will I get to work without a car tomorrow? I need this motherfucker up and running, god-damn it!"

I'm on the verge of tears when I hear Brody ask, "Do you have a blanket in there?"

I snap my head up at the question. "A blanket?"

He nods his head and points at the back seat. "Yeah, a blanket to cover the little guy, when I carry him to my car. I don't want him to get wet and catch a cold."

"I have a blanket," I say, and blink stupidly, but don't make a move to retrieve it.

"Well, where is it?" Brody asks slowly, as if I'm mentally impaired.

I snap to action and reach over to the side to get the small blanket and throw it over the car seat. Brody retreats the covered sleeping baby, and puts him in his car, so I close up my car and follow after him. I'm getting completely soaked with the now heavily pounding rain before I can even take two steps.

My body shivers when I place myself in the passenger seat of Brody's car and the heating starts blowing on my wet clothes. Brody puts the car in gear and soon turns in the opposite direction from where we live.

"Um, Brody? That's the wrong way, I live in the north part of the city..."

"I know," he grunts. "I'm taking you to my place. I think I have some cables in the garage. If it's really just the battery, then maybe we'll be able to get your car running. At least for some time. But if it's the alternator, then I won't be able to do much. I do have a friend who's a mechanic, but that would have to wait until tomorrow."

"I have work in the morning," I say glumly and sigh. "Maybe I should just call Gary, that I won't make it."

Brody hums in his throat but doesn't answer as he concentrates on the road. The storm is now in full swing, and I gulp when there's a lightning bolt flashing through the sky ahead of us.

The thunder must be what finally wakes Henry because I hear a wobbly, "Nanny?" from the back.

I turn to my son and smile with a fake cheer. "Hey, kiddo! You'll see granny pretty soon, okay? Now, we're going on a trip with Uncle Brody."

"Toy?" Henry asks and tries to see into the driver's seat.

"Hey, buddy," Brody calls to him and glances briefly over his shoulder. "Do you want to see where I live?"

Of course, like every time when being asked a question, Henry nods his head, not fully understanding what he agrees to.

When his eyelids start to drop again, I relax in my seat and smooth the leather of the upholstery in Brody's car.

"Good to see some things didn't change," I muse, then glance Brody's way, "I always thought your car fits your personality."

He frowns as the road gets harder, and harder to navigate, then asks, "And why is that?"

"Oh, please don't make me say it." I smile shyly, feeling my face getting a little flushed. Why did I have to open my big mouth?

"Wouldn't peg you for someone who's scared to speak her mind," he eggs me on, looking intrigued by my possible answer.

"You know, the whole... dark sexy macho thing," I respond, making him laugh.

"Is that how you see me?" he asks with a grin, and I groan while hiding myself in my hands.

"Come on, Jen. Don't be embarrassed. I'm just teasing you."

I lift my head and throw him a dirty look, that he doesn't even catch, as he slows down to avoid a fallen branch on the bumpy road. "Well, yeah, but it's embarrassing considering I had a ginormous crush on you back then."

"Did you?" he asks with fake shock and chuckles when I give him the finger.

"Shut up!" I protest and start laughing too. My laughter dies, however, when there's another boom resonating through the sky. I squish my face to the window to see better and frown at the surrounding conditions. "Uh, Brody? How much further are we going? I don't think the road will be drivable in a couple of minutes."

"Yeah, I didn't think it would get this bad. I would've just turned back to the shelter. But it's too late now. We're two minutes from my house, but it's going to be tricky. The area is pretty much uninhabited."

"Hmm," I hum in response and fold my arms, staying silent until we turn into a forest dirt road. "Where are you taking us? I swear I saw horror movies that started off like this. Are you going to chop me into little pieces with an axe in some shabby cabin in the middle of nowhere?"

"No."

"Cool. So, how much longer..." I stop in the middle of the sentence when a house appears in sight.

It's a modern-looking wooden cabin with plenty of windows, surrounded by tall trees, illuminated only by the small lights installed above the entrance. It looks like the perfect combination of rustic and contemporary. For a moment, I forget about our predicament and just stare at it through the rain-stained car window, as Brody clicks a button on his console to open the garage door.

"This is where you live?" I look back at him with wide eyes, motioning at the building as we drive toward the parking space inside.

"It is. You like?" Brody asks breezily and without a pause gets out to retrieve my bag and takes Henry out of the back.

I slap my hand on the roof of his car as I get out. "Do I? Brody, I never thought I'll say it about a building but, it's fucking beautiful." Then my eyebrows knit, and I falter in my step as a sudden thought hits me. "Wait. You live here on your own, right?"

"Yeah... Why?" He throws over his shoulder and leads me to a mudroom, where I take off my shoes.

"Oh, uh, just making sure." I nervously scratch at my hair, and follow after Brody. "You know... I wasn't sure how you're gonna explain my presence if you've got a wife stored in here that you didn't tell me about. Or a girlfriend." I cast him an uncertain look and then glance away quickly, biting my lip as he turns to look at me.

"No wife. No girlfriend," Brody states and opens the door that I guess leads to the living part of the house. "Come on in."

"Wow, Handsome. How did you find this place? Everything looks so.... Cozy," I say in astonishment as I look around.

We come through the side door into a sort of living room. The house is mostly an open plan, and it consists of a nice area with a sofa in front of the fireplace and a small coffee table nearby. Pictures and colorful art adorn the walls, and a small wooden desk in the corner is almost fully covered with something that looks like architectural plans and math sheets. To the right, there's a kitchen with wooden cabinets, a long counter, and a table that can fit four people. To the left, a door that I assume leads to a bathroom, and next to it a staircase. Behind it is a large glass door looking out at the backyard, but for now, all I see is the darkness getting split with more thunderbolts.

"It's nothing fancy, I guess. But I'm actually proud to admit I built it myself," Brody informs me, sounding almost self-conscious contrary to his words.

I whirl on him and smile excitedly. "Shut up! You did not! Brody, that is so wonderful," I gush and step further inside to inspect everything closely.

"Glad you approve. I made some of the furniture too," he says and watches me as I run my hand over the surface of the table, then clears his throat, and looks down at the sleeping baby he still cradles. "I don't think I ever saw a baby that would sleep like that. The kid is totally dead to the world. I think I got him a little wet from my shirt, do you have some change of clothes for him in the bag?"

"Yeah, is there a place where I can change him? Or..."

"Come on, I'll show you the guest room. I can bring something for you to change in too. You need to get out of those wet clothes, so you won't catch a cold. And I don't think we will be going anywhere until the road is drivable, so you may as well get comfortable," Brody says and climbs the stairs.

"Yeah, okay..." I murmur, trying to cast away my dirty thoughts as I follow him. Yes, we're alone. At his house. Forced to be close by the power of nature. What could go wrong?

Oh, yeah. Henry. Aaand the fact that Brody doesn't seem that excited about us being here. Good God, why must you put me to the test again?

CHAPTER XI

B rody
We go upstairs, where I show Jen to the guest room, and lie down sleeping Henry on the bed. "Go ahead, make yourself at home. You can change the kid here, and then take a shower in the adjoining bathroom if you like. I will find something for you to wear in that time and leave it on the bed here for when you're finished."

"Yeah, okay," Jen responds quietly, standing in the middle of the room, uncertainty written on her face. I want to think that she's not too uncomfortable about being here alone with me.

"Hey." I wait for her to focus on me before I continue. "I'm really sorry for dragging you both here, I thought we'll escape the storm. I... I'm glad that you're here, though. Not only that, but I'm glad that I was right behind you... you know, with the car." I stutter my words out like a nervous teenager and wince internally.

"Yeah, I'm glad too," Jen responds timidly and bites her lip. We stand like that and stare at each other, the air between us charged. I'm hit again with feelings that sneak up on me more and more lately. Feelings that I won't get a chance to explore.

Before I make an even bigger idiot out of myself or say too much, I slip out of the guestroom and go to my own bedroom. I sit on my bed with a heavy sigh and rub my neck.

"You stupid fucker," I whisper to myself, then listen to the sound of Jen's voice as she talks to Henry. I guess the little bugger finally woke up.

I didn't think about how hard it would be to have them here with me. About how much more it will make me dream of the things that I have no business wanting. Like Jen. Like having Jen in my space. Loving Jen. Creating a new family with Jen.

Those are the things I can't think of right now. Not when we've just reconciled. Not just weeks after she found out about her mother's murder. And certainly not with Henry's father still out there.

I overheard Jen's conversation with Amelia last week, where they talked about her getting calls from that fucker. I'm not sure what's the status there, but I won't be putting myself on the line if there's even the slightest chance that she'll be back with him when he gets out. Even if that's not the case, he's probably going to be in his kid's life, as well as Jen's, and I don't know how I feel about that.

On the one hand, I get that Jen's got a life and baggage that I would have to deal with when the time comes. If the time comes. But on the other hand, I feel possessive and jealous at the thought of having another man in her life. I know that's fucked up, and I am not entitled to wish that she was all mine with each and every aspect of her life happening in my sphere. But I was always a tangled mess when it came to her, and I don't think I will ever stop feeling so strongly about Jen.

I get up to get out of my wet shirt, and as usual, grimace at my reflection in the mirror next to my dresser. Here is another reason why I won't be acting on my romantic feelings toward Jennifer. Half of my torso and a large part of my right shoulder is now covered in uneven, ugly scars. I lift my hand to touch it and sigh at the unpleasantness of the bumpy skin.

I was never a shy person, or self-conscious about my looks before that day in the warehouse. People, mostly women, always told me how handsome I was, how great my body looked, and I never had an issue with intimacy. Yet since getting burned, I wasn't able to even consider getting naked in front of a woman.

When I hear the shower running next door, I snap out of it and pull on a fresh shirt before finding the smallest t-shirt and pants I own for Jen to wear. Before I open the door, I hesitate and listen to the sounds coming from the bathroom. I'm trying not to think about her naked body not even five feet away from me, but it's hard for me not to imagine her covered in soap, touching herself in the steam-filled cabin.

Glancing down at the bulge in my jeans, I hiss at my treasonous dick, "Calm the fuck down! This isn't the time for this." I shake my head in annoyance at myself. It's been too long since I've been with anybody, so it's no wonder I can't keep my mind out of the gutter.

After I'm finished counting to a hundred and thinking about everything gross I saw in life, I take a deep breath and march to the guest room. The water was still running when I left my room, but I still knock lightly before I enter.

I find the guestroom in a state of complete disarray, with a fully awake Henry sitting in the center of the mess, eating one of those dry biscuits that he likes. There's a phone on his lap displaying a vividly colored cartoon.

"Hey, little man. What happened here?" I ask and wait patiently for him to acknowledge me. After a few prolonged seconds, Henry lifts his head and looks at me, then around him.

"Mamma," he states with a nod and immediately concentrates back on the screen.

"Your mom did all this?" I ask with a chuckle.

Once again the kid looks up, this time with a heavy sigh, as if he's tired of my shit, and stresses, "Yes. Mamma do."

"Okay, okay. I believe you," I say in a serious tone. "Why don't we help a little with the clean-up, huh?"

Henry nods but comes back to whatever he's watching, dismissing me completely. I smile to myself and tap his little head before grabbing everything he's thrown out of the bag, probably searching for the snacks. When I hear the shower stall open, and Jen moving around in the bathroom, I quickly put everything on the bed, including the clothes I brought her, and get out of there as fast as I can.

It's already hard as it is – pun intended, no need to add the view of a half-naked Jen getting straight out of a shower to torment me even further.

"Jen? I left you something to wear. Come downstairs when you're ready," I call through the closed door.

"Okay!" she calls back, and I exhale loudly at hearing her sweet voice. Get a fucking grip, man.

I get downstairs and move to light up the fireplace. Normally, I wouldn't bother with it because I'm used to sleeping in lower temperatures, but I want Jen and Henry to feel comfortable and warm at my house.

I'm stacking the firewood, lost in thought, when I suddenly feel eyes on me. Turning around with a piece of wood in hand, I start asking, "Hey, did you..." and then almost choke on my own spit.

I turn into a coughing fit when I spot Jen standing barefoot in the middle of my living room, dressed in just my t-shirt that barely reaches her mid-thigh. Her toned long legs are on full display, and for the life of me, I can't stop my eyes from perusing them. I snap my head up to look at her face, and gulp at the sight of her wet hair hanging loosely around her beautiful face.

"Hey there. What are you doing?" Jen asks with a gleam in her eye.

"What?" I mutter stupidly, and blink down at the wood that I'm holding up. "Oh, I thought I'll light the fire. You know... in case you or Henry feel cold."

"Wow, and he's thoughtful. Damn Brody, hasn't anyone told you that men are supposed to have flaws?" she flirts as she comes closer.

"Believe me, baby, I have many of those," I respond absentmindedly, eyeing her legs once again, and then forcing myself to look away. I turn to the fireplace and focus on my task before asking, "So, uh, was there something wrong with the pants I gave you? I'm sure I can find something else for you to wear."

Jen steps next to me and smirks. "I tried them on, but honestly, I could fit my whole body in one leg of those pants. But don't worry, I'm quite comfortable like this." She gestures toward her body, making my mouth go dry as I involuntarily follow the movement from the corner of my eye.

"I bet you do," I grumble and poke at the slowly burning wood, before closing the cover and standing up. "Where's the little guy?"

"Well, after eating half a pack of biscuits, he passed out on the carpet. If that's not good parenting, I don't know what is," Jenny jokes and trails after me to the kitchen. "Little rascal. The second he's left alone, he comes rummaging through the bag, searching for the goodies."

"Shit, you could've told me to watch him for you," I say sheepishly, watching as Jen sits up on the kitchen counter. Don't look at her legs. Don't you look at her legs, you motherfucker.

She waves me off and laughs. "Nah, he'll be fine. God only knows what Rita has been up to with him when I leave for work. A little sugar won't kill him."

"Probably not." I chuckle and look out the window. The storm is starting to let up, but there's still heavy rain pounding on the windows. "I don't think we will be going to see your car today. It's getting late, and the road will be too muddy, so I'm afraid you're stuck here with me."

Jen glances in the direction I'm looking and sighs. "I figured. I've already called Gary that I won't be in tomorrow. He was cool about it, but I won't be able to come to Ruth's next Sunday because I will have to work off the missed day."

"Oh shit, I'm sorry, Jen. If I had known..."

She shakes her head and cuts me off with a smile. "It's fine, Brody. I wouldn't be able to get to work without my car anyway. And if I didn't wanna be here, I wouldn't. Storm or not."

"All right then." I smile back. "So, how about some wine before bedtime?"

"I would love to. I'm just going to check on Henry, and I'll be right back," Jenny jumps off the counter, and exits the kitchen with my eyes following her ass.

Fuck. Maybe that wine isn't a good idea.

I mentally slap myself and go looking through the cupboards for a nice bottle I know I have stored somewhere in here. Then pour two glasses and carry them to the living room just in time to see Jen coming down the stairs.

"He's dead to the world," she says happily and grabs the offered glass of wine before taking a small sip. She hums in appreciation and goes to look through the ginormous window I had installed to have a clear view of the surrounding nature.

"Is it normal for a kid his age to sleep so much?" I ask, truly curious.

Jen snorts and looks over her shoulder at me. "God, I wish. Henry is an early riser, and from the moment he wakes up, he's giving me and Rita hell. Well, mainly Rita because I'm usually absent in the mornings," she adds, looking a little sad, but then quickly shakes it off and continues. "I took him to a park this morning. He chased every duck he spotted. Poor thing wanted to give them a hug and couldn't understand why they didn't want his love."

With a chuckle, I move closer to her. We watch the rain and trees swinging in the wind, drinking wine in comfortable silence for a moment, before she says almost to herself, "A patio here would be great."

She takes one more sip of her wine, and after one final glance at the outdoors, moves further into the room to inspect the family photos I have hanging on the wall.

"You don't talk much about your past," she mutters, looking at the picture of a ten-years-old me between a proud-looking Ruth and her husband Frank. "Were you always living with them?"

"Hmm, no. They took me in when I was about eight. Ruth was my mother's sister," I tell her after coming closer to inspect the serious look on my boyish face, that I wore constantly from a young age.

"What about your parents?" Jen asks quietly.

I scratch at my neck, and sigh. "They, uh... they died in a car accident. My father was the driver. He was drunk."

Jen gasps and turns to me. "Brody, that's awful. I'm sorry. Where were you at the time?"

"I was with Ruth, thankfully. My parents left me with her a lot anyway, so my living situation didn't change that drastically after they passed. I guess you could say she was raising me anyway," I admit. "My parents liked to party, and they had me very young. I don't think they were ready to take on such a responsibility as taking care of a child."

Jen snorts. "That's a lame excuse for being a shitty parent, if I ever heard one."

I think about her story for a moment and have to agree. "You're right. I don't know why I feel the need to justify their neglect. Maybe age had nothing to do with it."

"I get it. Things like that aren't always black and white. They weren't perfect, but they were still your parents, and you loved them despite their flaws. Their actions didn't take away from the grief," Jen says gruffly, her eyes filling with tears.

Without thinking, I'm lifting my arm to put it around her shoulders before hugging her to my side. "I know right now these are just words, but I promise you that it will get better. It will get easier. The pain will stay with you. The loss. But it will lessen with time."

Jen exhales loudly before straightening to look me straight in the eyes. "I'm so glad that you're back in my life, Brody."

Her gaze starts moving toward my lips as something close to want appears on her face, and I swallow hard, my free hand moving instinctively toward the small of her back.

I open my mouth to say something just as thunder reverberates through the house, and I immediately step back as if electrocuted, almost tripping over my own feet.

I clear my throat and try to recover quickly, but I can already see Jenny's face transforming into a disappointed frown because of my reaction. "How about a refill?" I point at her almost empty glass.

She looks down at the glass she's holding with lowered eyebrows and shakes her head. "No, I... I think it's getting late. I should probably just..." Before I can react, she pushes the wineglass into my hand, mutters a half-assed "Goodnight," and climbs the stairs in a rush.

Her naked legs are the last thing I see before she disappears upstairs, with the sound of closing doors hitting me as if an invisible hand slapped me.

Jesus Christ, I can't believe I almost gave in. I was seconds from kissing her sweet little mouth. Seconds from tasting her and turning the fantasy into reality. And I know I wouldn't be able to stop. I'd be gone and going to hell for it.

It would be worth going to hell for, a small voice in my head whispers as I clear the glasses and put everything away before going to my bedroom.

CHAPTER XII

J enny
It's after midnight and I find myself staring at the ceiling and reminiscing everything that happened so far while I listen to the calming sounds of Henry's breathing and the house settling down after the storm.

The rain is still pattering gently on the roof window, but the moon has made its appearance some time ago, casting soft light onto the wooden floors.

I think about the moment I thought Brody was finally going to kiss me. He wanted it just as much as I did. I'm sure I didn't imagine it. But why is he always pushing me away at the last moment?

Now, I'm not naïve to think that a man like Brody would ever settle with a girl like me. That goes without saying. But the chemistry between us is undeniable, and I wish we could exploit it. At least until it's time for us to move on.

Feeling hot and bothered by the needs Brody awakened in me, I throw away the covers and fan myself with my hand. I feel frustrated and on edge.

Not able to deal with this restlessness, I peek one more time at the sleeping toddler, and then get out of bed before I can talk myself out of what I'm about to do. I exit the guest room and move blindly along the wall until I reach a doorknob.

Silently, I enter Brody's bedroom and make out his sleeping form in the moonlit room. I step soundlessly toward the bed and reach out with my hand to touch his face. Before I'm even halfway there, though, his hand shoots from under the covers at the speed of light, and he grabs my wrist before I can even blink. I'm being pulled forward and then flipped on the bed, so I land with Brody hovering over me, his hands restricting both of my wrists.

I gasp loudly at the feel of Brody's strong thighs around my own, and the sound brings Brody back from his attack mode. He shakes his head and leans back in shock.

"Jenny? What the hell? Did no one ever tell you to not creep on a sleeping former soldier? Fuck. I could've hurt you," he whispers angrily and breathes sharply before letting go of my hands. His legs stay in place, though, straddling me.

I don't answer him as I'm too busy perusing his perfectly sculpted chest, the moonlight illuminating one side of his body. Our eyes meet, and I pant when Brody tries to move away from my body but only ends up rubbing his hard dick, that's straining his cotton pajama pants, on my leg. I grab his forearms and stop him from moving further.

His brows furrow. "Jen, what are you..."

I shush him by putting my finger on his mouth and then, before he can protest, remove it and lift my head to close the distance between us in a kiss, making Brody groan. I move my head back slightly, putting my hands on his handsome face, and gaze straight into his eyes as I whisper against his lips, "Please, don't reject me. I know you want this."

Brody doesn't move, stiff as a statue as he whispers back with a strained face. "Baby, we can't. It's wrong."

"No, it's not," I argue sternly and move to kiss him on the neck, smirking when he growls loudly and clenches his fists by my side, trying to restrain himself from touching me.

Then I move to the other side of his neck and slide my palm down his chest. "Don't think. Just feel." And just as I say that, I feel the uneven crevices on the side of Brody's torso, that's covered by the shadow.

Before he can move away, I lean forward and kiss the rough, scarred skin. Brody tries to protest, but when I shove my hands down his boxers, all I get from him is a sharp intake of breath.

Just as my hand curls around his hard shaft, he grabs it to stop me, and protests weekly, "Jen, I don't want to take advantage of you."

I lift myself again to meet his gaze before kissing him softly. "You won't, I want this." And then I draw my lips closer to his ear to whisper desperately, "Fuck me, Brody."

"Christ," he says through clenched teeth, but grabs my hips in his hands and moves my body closer to his. He gazes into my eyes as if trying to gauge my reaction to his touch and then seems to finally make up his mind when he mutters, "Guess I'm going to hell," before kissing me hungrily.

Our tongues intertwine as we both recline on the bed, Brody's weight on me, his dick aligning perfectly between my open thighs. One of Brody's hands tangles in my hair, while the other one moves south, touching my breast through the goddamn t-shirt. Why do we still have clothes between us?

Just as I think it, Brody grabs the hem of my shirt and moves back to remove it with a little help from me. Then he lowers his head down to capture one of my nipples in his mouth and sucks lightly, making me moan. The sound spurs him on, and he takes his other hand to reach down after he releases my nipple from his mouth, only to switch to the other.

He grabs one of my things and lifts it slightly before trailing slowly toward my pussy and when his fingers touch my folds, he lifts his head and breathes, "Fuck you're so wet."

"Just fucking touch me already," I pant, turned on more than I've ever been in my entire life.

Brody groans again, "You're killing me, woman." Then kisses me and starts rubbing my pussy with expert hands, my body jerking when he reaches my clit.

"Yes, Brody. Please. More." I gasp unabashedly and then cry out in pleasure when his fingers enter me.

"Fuck. You're so tight, baby," he whispers in between kisses.

When I can't take the teasing anymore, being on the constant edge of orgasm, I wail impatiently in between moans, "God damn it, stop playing and fuck me already!"

Brody chuckles darkly and then asks, "Fuck you?" as he suddenly moves back and stares at me intently. His hands stop moving and I growl in frustration.

"Do you really want it, Jen? Because if we do this, there's no going back. So, I'm only going to ask this once, and then all bets are off. Do you want me?" he asks slowly, the expression on his face more serious than I ever saw him.

For a moment, I get lost in his eyes and hesitate, but then whisper, "Yes, I want you, Brody."

"Thank fucking God," he mutters with relief and grabs my face to press our lips together in a passionate kiss. His body crushes mine into the mattress, making me feel small and feminine as he dominates me. When my hands roam his back to reach his boxers, he lifts his hips and without parting our lips, we cooperate to remove the obstacle, and then without any preamble Brody enters me in one swift motion, making me cry out a little too loud.

"Are you okay?" he whispers and removes the hair from my face to look at me with concern.

"Yeah. Just... you're bigger than I'm used to," I admit and blink up at him.

Brody's jaw tenses, and he says in a husky voice, "Baby, the flattery will get us nowhere right now. Please tell me you're all right. Because if I don't move soon, I swear I'm gonna lose my mind. You feel so good."

I kiss his jaw and say, "Yes, please move."

He withdraws a little just to push back in, and I moan, already adjusting to his size. We both move in a steady rhythm, our bodies aligning perfectly, my orgasm building up with each slam. When yet again I am almost on the verge and feel myself getting strung up, Brody sits back, kneeling on the bed as he swiftly takes me with him, lifts me by the hips in the air like I weigh nothing, and impales me on his cock faster and faster.

I clutch the sheets in my hands and breathe a loud curse, when Brody hits the perfect spot, making me combust, my whole body shaking. I gasp in surprised ecstasy when I'm not even fully down from my first climax, and Brody lifts his thumb to lick it and then presses it to my clit, making me orgasm a second time. Holy fuck!

After I mutter out a string of nonsense, trashing in the bed like I'm possessed, Brody picks up his pace and soon after grunts out his own release before collapsing next to me on the bed. He flips to his back and tucks me into his chest, his erratic breaths tickle my hair when he kisses me sweetly on the forehead.

"You're all right, sweetheart?"

"All right?" I incline my head to meet his gaze. "I think you ruined me, Brody."

"In a good way, I hope." He chuckles.

I lift myself to kiss him and mutter, "In the best way," before settling on his chest again and drawing lazy patterns across his exposed torso.

"We probably should take a shower," I yawn. "We're both dirty and sweaty."

"Yeah," he mutters, but doesn't make a move to get up, as he starts playing with my hair. I don't remember ever feeling that way in someone's arms.

I smile to myself, but it soon melts off my face as I look around the dark bedroom and feel the warm, beautiful body that is supporting my weight. It makes me feel like an impostor in someone else's life. Like I don't belong in his story. Like it shouldn't be me lying here with this remarkable man. I so do not deserve him. I'm spoiling the picture of perfectness. Goddamn it.

"If you think any louder, you're gonna wake up the neighbors," Brody drawls lazily.

"How far is your closest neighbor from here? I didn't see any houses around while we were driving."

"Far. So, that's precisely my point." Brody removes his arm and turns to the side, so we're lying face to face. He tucks a piece of my hair behind my ear and then surveys my face with a soft expression. "What's running through that head of yours?"

"It's just that..." I hesitate but then go for it. "Why don't you have a wife or a girlfriend living here with you?"

I don't know what Brody thought my response would be, but I can see my question caught him off guard. He blinks twice slowly and bites the inside of his cheek before he answers. "I'm not sure what you are asking here exactly. Do you want me to have a wife or a girlfriend?"

"What? No. I mean..." I roll my eyes and gesture toward his face. "You're all... that. And you have the house, the car, you're the nicest person I know, and you have a big dick..." The last one makes him grin, but then he smooths his expression and waits for me to continue. "Why don't you have some gorgeous woman strutting around pregnant with your fourth offspring? Why would a flawless and handsome guy be here all on his own and then allow a fucking stray like me under his roof?"

With each of my words, Brody's eyebrows rise higher with surprise, but when I finish, he looks downright furious.

"What the fuck, Jen? Is this how you see this?" He motions between us. "Me taking in a stray to my bed? Fucking said stray because I have nothing else to do? Binding my time until someone else comes along? Fuck!"

I flinch back a little and cover myself when Brody sits up abruptly, breathing harshly. I know he wouldn't hurt me, but old habits die hard. I do it unconsciously, but of course, he notices and my reaction makes him even angrier. He shakes his head with disgust and mutters, "Fucking great," before getting out of bed and grabbing his discarded underwear from the floor.

I sit up quickly and demand, "Where the fuck are you going? I was only curious, okay? I'm sorry!"

I lower my voice remembering that Henry sleeps next door, and repeat, "I'm sorry, Brody."

Brody puts his pajama bottoms on, then hangs his head with a heavy exhale.

I find my T-shirt in the dark room and put it on before walking hesitantly toward Brody. I stop right in front of him and tilt my head, so I can find his gaze. I take one of his hands in mine and pull it gently with a shy smile. "Hey, I'm sorry if I stepped out of line. I won't ask again."

Instead of the smile I'm anticipating, I receive an even more displeased expression marring his face before he laughs indignantly.

I drop his hand in surprise and step back, but Brody grabs me before I can retreat and presses me to his body.

"Jesus Christ, you make me mad, woman." He shakes his head and kisses my forehead before looking straight at me, his eyes narrowed. "Jen, you can ask me whatever you want, whenever you fucking feel like it. You don't ever have to be scared of questioning me or demanding anything." When he sees my doubtful expression, he takes me by the shoulders and squeezes me gently, and then states forcefully, "What does make me fucking furious though is you speaking about yourself in a derogatory way. Or you thinking that you're not important to me. Because, baby, if I haven't been obvious enough about it, then let me assure you. You are important to me."

I stare at him, not knowing what to say, and blink at him like an idiot.

"And to address your question, before you come up with more stupid shit in your head, the reason I don't have a wife or a girlfriend here is that I don't allow just anyone into my house. There's a small number of people I care about in this world. This space is mine, and it's reserved for only the important ones. Since I never met a woman before worthy of such a privilege until you, it never happened. Moreover, I've been kind of preoccupied with a certain pain in the ass."

He slides his hands from my shoulders to the back of my neck, squeezing lightly. "Does that answer your question, Jen?"

I nod slowly and swallow, not knowing if I want to wail or throw myself at him. Unwilling to ruin the moment with my tears as I unpack everything that was said, I decide on the latter and kiss Brody hard, surprising him with the motion, if his startled hum is anything to go by.

We make out for some time and then decide to clean up together in the bathroom. I check on Henry, who managed to kick off his blanket in his sleep, but otherwise didn't even change his position, and I go back to a half-asleep Brody. I curl into his warm, strong arms and quickly fall asleep. For the first time, dreaming about things unrelated to my past.

It's one week later as I drive my newly repaired car like a mad woman through the curvy dirt road before stopping right in front of Brody's house, still in my waitress uniform.

I knock on the door impatiently and almost fall into Brody in my haste to get inside.

"Come on in," he says sarcastically, still dressed in his work clothes. I halt in my step and eye the paint-stained jeans, black steel-toed boots, and an unbuttoned flannel shirt. Damn, Brody is always hot but this... I have no words.

"Sweetheart, not that I'm not happy to see you, but what...?" He stops in the middle of the question when I reach to the back of my dress and unzip it. The material pools at my feet, leaving me only in black underwear.

"I gave Rita money to take care of Henry for two extra hours. Since it took me," I look down at my watch, "twenty-five minutes to get here, I would say we have a little more than an hour to enjoy ourselves," I finish and look at him expectantly.

Brody eyes me and licks his lips but stays in place. "I..."

"Unless you're not up for it. I know at your age..." I don't get to finish because I'm being lifted in the air and thrown over Brody's shoulder in a blink of an eye. I yelp in protest, and then again when I feel a hard slap on my exposed ass just as we're starting to move up the stairs.

"Brody! Put me down!" I say, but it's laced with my gleeful giggles when my body swishes upside down on his backside.

"This will happen every time you test me," Brody says calmly, his voice is laced with humor.

We enter the bathroom, and I'm being disposed of on the cold countertop.

"So, that would mean always because I'm all about testing you, big guy," I smart with a sultry smile.

Brody grins and leans toward my face with a grin. "And I'm here for it," and then taps my nose before turning around to start the shower.

Okay, I always loved broody Brody with his dark looks and scowling face, but I think I may love playful and sweet Brody even more. Whom am I kidding? That man is always sexy, regardless of what he does.

After Brody makes sure the temperature in the shower is right, he undresses, with me thoroughly enjoying the free show, and after I step out of my underwear, we both get into the big shower stall.

We start cleaning each other's bodies, and although it starts innocent enough, soon I end up kneeling on the wet tiles and taking Brody into my mouth, groaning at the feel of his hard cock touching the back of my throat. I suck hard, relentlessly until he starts losing control, groaning and cursing, his grip on my hair getting tighter. I open my eyes to look up at his beautiful face and meet his passion-filled gaze.

"Come here." He breathes and slides away from between my lips to lift me. My legs wrap around his hips, so Brody's cock can easily slide inside. I lean my back on the glass shower wall and get a hold of a metal handle, hanging on for dear life as Brody starts pounding into me powerfully, hard and fast, and I know he had to be restraining himself last week because this man fucking me right now is a beast.

After he repositions us a little and starts hitting that spot deep within, I cry out loudly and my eyes roll into the back of my head in ecstasy. Soon my whole body feels like fire is enveloping me, and my trembling hands let go of the shower stall as I come. Thankfully, before I fall, Brody takes a better hold of me and supports my weight fully as he changes the rhythm to a slower one and orgasms with a soft curse on his lips.

Because I didn't fully regain control of my limbs yet, Brody washes the both of us again before we exit the shower and towel off.

My body feels positively spent as I gather my underwear and hum a happy song, unconscious of the fact Brody is watching me.

His waist is wrapped in a towel as he leans on the counter with a soft smile and says, "I love seeing you like this."

I wipe the fog from the mirror above the sink and look at my wet hair in a state of complete disarray with a grimace. "Like what?"

"Like happy, and free."

I look back at him and respond shyly, "You do tend to make me feel that way, Handsome." Then I look at my watch and mutter, "But all nice things must come to an end. I'll need to get going soon."

Brody seems to think that over before he clears his throat. "You know, we wouldn't have to rush or make plans, or go to such extremes like paying Rita to watch Henry, just so we could spend some time together if you were both here."

"Here?" I step back from the vanity and concentrate on Brody's stern face. "What do you mean?"

He scratches his head and looks away before straightening from the counter. "You know, I've been thinking about this.

About us. I know it's probably too fast, but how would you feel about..."

"No," I refuse strongly before he can propose anything.

"What do you mean, no? You haven't even heard what I was about to say, I mean we could at least talk about it so we know where we stand," he says and frowns at the panicked look on my face. "I know it's early, and we never got a chance to talk about what we are and what the future holds..." Brody stops when I start shaking my head vehemently.

"What we are? Future?" I laugh jeeringly. "Brody, with me there's no future! I have a baggage the size of Canada. We could just have fun. There's no need to overcomplicate things between us," I plead.

"Overcomplicate?" he asks in a low voice, then throws, "Then you should've thought about that before you overcomplicated things and jumped on my dick! What the fuck is wrong with you?"

I gasp in offense and my sight smudges with unshed tears. "I didn't jump..."

"Yes, you fucking did!" Brody points at my face, looking hurt and furious. "I was trying to stay the fuck away, to be your goddamn friend. I told myself you're unreachable. Not for me. But then you came to my bed. My fucking bed! Looking beautiful and whispering into my ear. I lost my damn mind, Jen. But I asked you. I fucking asked you! Do. You. Want. Me?" He slaps the counter with each yelled word, and I step back.

"But you're a goddamn liar, aren't you?" he continues, breathing harshly through his nose. "You don't want me. So, what was this about, then? What are we doing here then if there's no us, and there can't be even a conversation about a potential future together? Huh?"

"I don't know..." I whisper, blinking rapidly. I can't believe that only a couple of minutes ago I was in heaven. Because now, seeing the wounded look on Brody's face mixed with disgust is pure and utter hell.

"You don't know," he snorts and crosses his arms. "Was I just meant to be your toy until your boyfriend gets out of jail?"

"What? No! Brody, of course not!" I grouse, distressed, and come closer to untangle his arms and grab his hand. I look into his eyes and say, "Ricky and I were done even before he went to jail. He's been calling, trying to reconcile, but I would rather die than be with this man again. Truly. However, he is Henry's father, so I can't exactly cross him out of my life if he wants to co-parent someday. I wouldn't hold my breath, though."

When Brody doesn't respond, I sigh and squeeze his hand. "Look, I'm sorry. But you know me. You know I'm not good enough. Would you really want me as your girlfriend? It would be only a matter of time before I fuck it all up. I don't know the first thing about a relationship. Can't we just have fun for some time?"

"Fun for some time?" Brody repeats unemotionally. "And then what?"

I smile at him wobbly and respond, ignoring the pang in my chest. "You find someone better, and I'll be on my way."

Brody drops my hand, and closes his eyes with a silent, "Jesus Christ." Then he looks down at me with a cold expression I remember well from that day in front of the police station. "I think you should go."

"Oh. Uh." The sadness, clutching me by the throat, prevents me from speaking for a moment. "Will you... uh, come by the diner this week, or..."

"Not likely," he says gruffly, then turns away, and walks past me saying, "You know where the door is," before he's gone. I hear his bedroom door being slammed shut, and it's what breaks the dam on my tears.

Knowing that I've already extended my stay here, I turn on my heel to get out. I run down the stairs and collect my dress from the floor, then throw it on, not even bothering with the zipper. I pull on my flats, and I'm out the door in a second.

As soon as I'm inside my car, I start sobbing uncontrollably, but don't let it stop me as I stomp on the accelerator a get the fuck away.

How do I always manage to destroy everything positive in my life?

CHAPTER XIII

The whole next week I have been miserable, walking around with a black cloud hanging over my head. My mood constantly swings from angry to sad and confused. And I hate this.

I hate the injustice of being treated like that by Brody, but what I hate even more is the fact that I miss him, and secretly hope for him to call, text, or to stop by.

Of course, my heart twists with disappointment each time I check the phone, and the only thing awaiting me there are unanswered calls from a private number, which I know to be Ricky's attempts to reach me.

Rita has been on my ass constantly about going to his parole hearing next month to present myself as the doting girlfriend and a mother of Ricky's child, begging for her man to be released, so we could finally be one happy family.

I usually just laugh it off and move on, entirely ignoring her threats about kicking me out. I've been hearing it for months, and I know these are just empty promises. She's not going to get rid of her personal piggy bank, or cast away Henry, who seems to be the only joy in her life right now. But I will admit that her pushing on the subject starts getting on my nerves, which doesn't improve my already shitty mood.

Today, though, is the first time that I felt slightly better and excited about my day from the moment I woke up in the morning. I tell myself that it has nothing to do with the fact today is Sunday and I will get to see Brody, and everything to do with the time I had to spend with my son. I mean, I do enjoy playing with Henry, but I will admit that he is not the reason I spent an extra-long time in front of the mirror choosing my outfit and doing my makeup for the first time in forever.

My palms shake as I park outside of Ruth's and I feel the first wave of uncertainty when I don't spot Brody's car anywhere. Maybe he parked in the back alley. It wouldn't be the first time. I mean, he has to be here, Aunt Ruth wouldn't let him miss the Sunday dinner.

I repeat that to myself when I get out of the car, and he doesn't show up to help me unclasp Henry from his seat, like he always does. What did I expect? The man literally kicked me out of his house only a few days ago.

That's fine. Maybe it'll allow me more time to compose myself for when I see him. Honestly, I don't know what my goal here is, but I feel the need to be in his presence. What for exactly? No idea. To make him face what he's lost? To exact an apology from him for wanting to be in a relationship with me? Yeah... that won't happen.

I'm so lost in the chaos inside my head that it gets me a moment to acknowledge that Amelia is standing right in front of me. I didn't even realize that she and Mark parked next to my car, and that they were both looking at me with concerned expressions.

"Hey, girlie." Amelia grabs my hand to draw my attention, then addresses her fiancé. "Mark, be a sweetie and help Jenny with Henry. Don't forget his bag."

"No, I can..." I say and frown over my shoulder when the heavily pregnant woman starts dragging me toward the entrance.

"He'll be fine. I heard Brody's not coming, so he's not here to help you. Have you lost some weight or is my perspective broken because all I see when I'm looking in the mirror is a whale-sized human being," she teases, but I see the concern in her eyes.

"I might have skipped some meals this week... Hey, why won't Brody show up?" I ask, aiming at casual. "I thought Ruth told him once, that if he misses the Sunday dinner, he'd better be on his deathbed, or she'll put him into one."

Amelia chuckles and leads us toward the kitchen. "Yeah, I guess something really important came up at the construction site, so she made an exception. Aren't you guys... talking?"

I scratch behind my ear and look away. "I guess we've all been busy lately."

My pregnant friend hums in her throat and gives me a calculating look but drops the subject when we enter the room to be greeted by a cheery-looking Ruth.

"There you are! My God Jenny, don't you look especially beautiful today." She kisses me on the cheek and peruses me as usual in her motherly way. "You're way too skinny, dear. But don't you worry, there's plenty of food to rectify that."

"Where are my girls? I thought they'll be waiting for their mama, tears in their eyes at the door," Amelia asks Ruth, looking around.

"Oh, yeah. Where's Sammy and Silvia?" I ask, only now noticing that they didn't arrive with Amelia and Mark.

"We had a sleepover last night!" Ruth answers me excitedly, looking like a giddy little girl for a moment. "I don't remember the last time I had so much fun. I can't wait for Henry to get a bit bigger, and for you to pop me more of those grandchildren, so we could have more happy times like this. I swear, even my Frank stopped being an old grumpy fart for one evening."

I choke on my own spit and start coughing as my eyes feel with tears.

"Jesus Christ, Ruth, that was so heavy-handed!" Amelia admonishes the older woman as she slaps me on the back.

Just as I start straightening, taking big gulps of air, the door opens and Mark walks in with a smiling Henry in his arms, and both girls trailing after him. When they notice their mom, they run over to her and squeeze each side of her giant stomach with happy squeals.

"So, you did miss me, huh? How was the slumber party at Aunt Ruth's?" Amelia asks with a tender smile.

Both girls start to excitedly shout over each other to share their adventures, making the adults laugh, with me joining in when I finally manage to regulate my breath.

I take Henry from Mark and take a seat at the table, watching the happy family interact with each other. A wave of sadness crashes into me at the realization that I will never get to experience that.

"Alright, now that we're all here, let's eat!" Ruth exclaims and gets busy serving everyone.

I get lost in thought again, and rest my chin on Henry's head, half-listening to the surrounding chatter, when Amelia's whisper reaches my ear. "Are you okay?"

"Yeah, sorry. Just tired," I murmur back and pretend to get interested in what's on my plate.

Truth be told, the food has been the last thing on my mind lately, but to avoid uncomfortable questions about my sour mood, I pretend to enjoy it. I smile throughout the dinner when everyone laughs, and nod when needed, but in reality I'm miles away.

I just finished feeding Henry, when Amelia stands up from her chair. "There's... a thing I left upstairs the last time I was here. I need to get it. Jenny, would you be so kind and help me climb the stairs?" she asks with an innocent smile and rubs her ginormous belly.

Mark, who's already getting up, starts, "I can..." but is quickly shut down when Amelia throws him a look and sits back down.

"Jenny will help me. Won't you?" the small woman asks, but it's not really a question. More like a command.

I glance down at Henry, then focus on Ruth, who's already been watching me. Her expression switches from thoughtful to polite as soon as our eyes meet.

"Will you take him? It appears that I have been summoned," I say, and hand him over. Then I follow after the heavily pregnant woman with my head hanging low.

I'm not even surprised when she starts easily climbing the steps without waiting for me. As soon as I hit the upper level, she drags me into a small room with cleaning supplies.

"Okay. Spill," she demands.

"What do you mean?" I ask impatiently and cross my arms.

"Jenny, I've known you for a while now. I hope that you consider me your friend. At least that's what you are to me," Amelia responds, looking vulnerable.

"Of course, we're friends," I say right away.

She nods, and continues, "Then as your friend, it pains me to see you this miserable. I saw Brody two days ago, he wasn't any better. What happened? Did you guys fight?" When she notices the expression on my face, her eyebrows lower in confusion. "I thought you two were pretty close. It can't be that bad."

I lick my lips and confess quietly, "We slept together."

My cheeks hit involuntarily, and I rub them with a groan when Amelia grins. "Oh my God! When?"

"It was happening for like a week until he kicked me to the curb," I admit.

My friend blinks at me slowly, and then asks with a skeptical face, "Damon? Kicked you to the curb? I don't believe that."

I roll my eyes and snort. "Well, he did. And now he doesn't want to see me, which he made pretty obvious by not coming here today to see me wear fucking makeup especially for him, together with this stupid ridiculous dress that I bought with the money I don't have. All because he thinks he wants to be with me and overcomplicate things between us with unnecessary feelings that could destroy something nice that we could have!" I almost yell out the last words and breathe harshly at the end of my tirade.

"Whoa, girl. There's a lot to unpack here. Start from the beginning please because I feel like I've missed something," Amelia says and sits on an overturned bucket getting comfortable before she puts one next to her and pats it. "Sit."

I take a seat and reluctantly recount everything that took place, starting with my car breaking down in the rain and finishing with Brody telling me to get lost.

"So, now I miss him like hell, and dream about getting back together with him, but at the same time I know my stance would be the same." I groan and tap my forehead.

"You know. I broke up with Mark right after I found out I was pregnant," Amelia tells me casually, and I snap my head up to look at her.

"Yep. You heard right." She laughs. "You remember how I used to be. Scared of my own shadow. Unable to function. When I met Mark, it was all so new, and scary. The thought of ruining his life by being... well, me, was unbearable. And you know what my ex did to me. I didn't think I could function in a relationship. I thought it was happening too soon."

"So, what did you do?"

"I stayed," she states with a nod.

I tilt my head to the side and parrot, "Stayed?"

"Yes. I owed it to myself to try. For me, for Mark, and for our baby," she says with a soft smile.

"But you see, that's the thing. You're both perfect. You create this perfect couple, and it comes to you so easy. I don't know the first thing about a healthy relationship."

This time, Amelia snorts, and I look at her in surprise. "Jenny, there's no such thing as perfect. Let's get that out of the way. And it doesn't come easy. Not at all. We have our ups and downs. All people do. And I didn't know what a relationship is supposed to look like either. Maybe even less than you do. But what I found out is that there's no special formula to make a good relationship. There's nothing to know. It's not a test you come prepared for. All it takes is a man that cares for you and respects you, and for you to reciprocate that. That's all. That's the big secret that most people search for."

"But he could have anyone," I protest weakly.

"Exactly. No offense." She waves a hand when I squint at her. "Yet he chose you. The why is really not important. He clearly cares about you deeply, Jenny. Sure, maybe he shouldn't jump on you with all of this after one week, and he sure shouldn't kick you out rather than talk this through to understand your perspective. But I came to know Damon pretty well, and the one thing I can say about the man is that he doesn't believe in half measures. If he's in, he's all in. If he's out, there will be no coming back."

"Yeah, I kind of got that last part," I grouse, and sigh. "I guess him not showing up today is a pretty good indicator of where his head's at."

"I wouldn't be so sure about that. Maybe he does need time to cool off, but he wouldn't lie to Ruth about the reason he's absent, and I heard them talking yesterday about some troubles with the house he's been working on."

"Oh, I didn't realize," I mutter, feeling stupid for making assumptions that it's all about me. And, I guess that's a good reminder that I don't have the monopoly on everyday struggles in life.

"Come on, help me up. My legs went to sleep in this position," Amelia whines as she tries to lift herself from the bucket, and I jump to my feet to help her.

"I think Henry and I will head out soon. I'll continue to be a shitty company for today's evening, anyway. And, honestly, maybe I should chew over everything in peace." We exit the storage room and move toward the staircase. "I'm still mad at Brody, but I may have been in the wrong too about this whole relationship thing."

"You think?" Amelia teases as we start to descend the stairs. "We'll probably hit the road soon too. This baby of mine is eating away at every last bit of my energy supplies. I swear all I could do is sleep. And the girls need to get ready for school tomorrow."

We walk into the kitchen just as Ruth puts two Tupperware containers full of food on the table and turns to me with a sugary sweet smile. "Oh, there you are. Jenny, I have a big favor to ask."

"What is it?" I ask tentatively, and then suspiciously eye the older woman when her smile stretches even further before her face changes into one of fake concern.

"Would you be so kind to deliver this to Damon?" She waves at the prepared containers. "My poor boy has been so busy this week with work, I worry about his bad eating habits. He's probably living on fast food, or God forbid, those dreadful frozen pizzas. I would be forever grateful if you would do that for me." She clasps her hands in a praying gesture, and it takes everything in me not to roll my eyes. Ruth's many things, but she's not winning an Oscar for the best actress anytime soon.

"What about Mark and Amelia? Don't they live closer to that part of the city?" I motion at the couple and notice the look Ruth throws their way.

Mark clears his throat, and steps forward. "I'm afraid, we can't." He glances at Amelia and nods. "She's dead on her feet. It's probably best if we drive straight home."

I look toward the ceiling with hands on my hips and exhale loudly, before focusing back on Ruth. "Okay. I'll bring Brody the food but know that you aren't being sleek. Neither are you." I point at Mark, who smirks.

"Oh, I don't know what you mean by that comment, but I'm glad for your help." Aunt Ruth smiles.

"Uh-huh. Let me just grab Henry's things then and I'll be on my way."

Ruth stops me in my tracks before I can reach the bag, and says, "No need, dear. I would love for him to stay if you'll allow it." When I look up at her with uncertainty written on my face, she comes closer and pleads, looking sincere. "I know you're very protective of him, but I swear I would be so happy to watch him for a while. I had so much fun with the girls last night, it reminded me of how much I missed because I couldn't have children of my own..."

I don't know if she's serious or if I'm being played, but I guess I can't say no after that confession.

"Fine. But I'll be back for him soon," I say with conviction, and then laugh when the woman jumps happily and squeezes my middle with surprising strength.

"Thank you, dear. And if you won't make it here tonight because of... unexpected events, I'll take care of Henry until you can pick him up tomorrow."

I look at her incredulously and say, "You're so full of shit, Ruth."

"Watch your language, young lady. Go kiss that baby of yours goodbye and off you go. The dinner is getting cold," she complains with a cunning smile.

I turn around and this time can't stop my eyes from rolling, but do as I'm told. After I make sure Henry is content with the situation, I pack the food containers and get out before the courage leaves me.

As I head toward Brody's cabin, I almost turn around twice, scared of what I will have to face when I get there.

Will he be happy to see me? Or will he tell me to get the fuck out again?

When I see the house appear between trees at the end of the rocky road, I tell myself that there's only one way to find out.

I barely manage to get out of the car and extract the bag with the food, when the door to the cabin opens. I falter in my step when I see Brody leaning on the door frame, dressed in his work clothes – similar to the ones he had on the last time I saw him. His posture is casual, but his face is completely emotionless as he watches me. I eye him from head to toe and gulp. Damn, why does he have to look so good?

As I step closer, I notice the weary lines on his face. He seems tired.

When I step right in front of him, he doesn't make a move to greet me or to let me in, just continues staring at me with this empty face that I fucking hate.

Momentarily I get unreasonably angry, and before I can think, my mouth opens. "Hi, Jenny, thanks for stopping by. Oh, you brought me food? That's so nice of you. You didn't have to do that, considering I kicked your ass out right after we fucked because you didn't want to do something I wanted."

Brody blinks at me once, but still, his face doesn't change, and if possible, it makes me even angrier, so I continue with this mockery. "Guess what, I told you that I care enough for you to move in with me, but as soon as we disagree on one thing, you're out. I won't call, I won't text, as if you never actually mattered at all. But it's all your fault, after all, it's you who jumped on my dick when I was defenseless and vulnerable, sleeping and minding my own business..."

I don't get to finish the sentence because before I can even think about my next words, I'm being dragged by my jacket into the house, and slammed against the front door. The bag I was holding drops at my feet with a bang, and I gasp in surprise before Brody's mouth attacks mine.

Without preservation, I kiss him back just as hungrily and moan in my throat when his hand lands at the bottom of my dress and grabs at my thigh.

As if I were trained to do that, I immediately lift my other leg to put it around his hips, and we both groan when his hardness hits my already wet core.

We start groping at each other, both spurred on by anger and desperation, and I cry out with pleasure when Brody swiftly moves my panties to the side and puts his fingers inside me.

My hips move on their own accord trying to create more friction, and I shamelessly moan, "Please..."

"Please, what..." Brody grunts into my ear after he bites my neck lightly.

"Please, fuck me," I moan.

Without hesitation, he unzips his pants and removes his fingers, only to slide his hard dick inside of me. We both moan loudly, and then Brody moves back to look me in the eyes before he rearranges us and grabs me lightly by the neck, while his other hand supports my weight.

Then he starts slamming into me full force, my back hitting the door every time, and it's the most out-of-body experience I've ever had.

It's not long before my eyes roll into the back of my skull and I yell out my release, the sound echoing around the cabin.

Over the fog in my brain, I hear Brody muttering a string of curses as he speeds up and comes inside me soon after.

We stay entangled like this for a while, trying to calm our breaths. Brody's face stays in my neck, and he gives me a small kiss before he backs away, and puts me down slowly.

My legs feel like Jell-O, and I have to lean on the door to stay up. I rearrange my clothes, and clear my throat, feeling so awkward after what we just did. "I, uh, can I use your bathroom? I need to... clean up," I ask the wall because I can't even face Brody.

From the corner of my eye, I see Brody watch me before he nods, and I don't waste any time before I almost run upstairs and straight into the bathroom.

I clean myself the best I can and fix my wild hair, all the time trying to ignore the shame and fear I have brewing inside of me.

Isn't that what I wanted? For him to use me for fun? I ask as I stare at myself in the mirror.

Jesus Christ, what the fuck is wrong with me? I told the guy that I didn't want a relationship with him, and pretty much proposed being friends with benefits, but the moment I actually think about it, I feel sick to the stomach.

My eyes widen when the realization hits me. Shit. I love him. I'm in love with him.

I don't want him to find some other woman one day who will show him real love, and will strut around pregnant with his baby. I want to be that fucking woman. I want his love and the life with him.

What if it's too late? No, no now that my mind feels clearer than ever before, I can't let the possibility of true happiness pass me by. I'm going to fight.

With that in mind, I head back downstairs, breezing by the door to grab the discarded bag that still lies on the floor. I'm relieved to see that nothing spilled out, and walk into the kitchen, where Brody leans on the kitchen counter, drinking a beer and looking into the distance with a thoughtful expression.

When he senses my presence, he puts the bottle away and takes a step toward me.

"I'm sorry..."

"I wanted to..." We speak at the same time, and I smile shyly. "Maybe you want to eat before we can talk. Ruth told me you had some issues lately and sent me here with reinforcements." I lift the bag.

Brody's eyebrows climb up on his forehead as he looks at it, and without a word, he walks toward the fridge. My jaw drops when he opens it, and each of the shelves appears to be stocked with containers.

"She already dropped by a few times. Including this morning, so..." He smirks and comes to retrieve the bag from me before putting it away with the rest of the food.

"That sneaky little..." I murmur and shake my head.

"Yeah, I'm not even surprised she pulled that." He chuckles, and the sight of his wonderful smile feels like a mouthful of cold water after being stranded in a desert for a week. Damn, I really missed him.

"Well, I felt like I was being played, but still..." I look away for a moment and then clear my throat. "I'm glad she did that, though. I think we ought to talk."

Brody nods, his face turning more serious before he asks if I want something to drink. I decide on a glass of wine and observe him moving around the kitchen as he pours it, and takes a beer for himself before sitting opposite me at the dining table.

I take three big gulps of the red liquid for courage, then say, "I guess, I'll go first. I'm truly sorry for how I reacted that day, Brody. You took me by surprise, and I wasn't ready to hear what you had to say. But I guess... I guess I'm ready to hear it now... If you want, that is," I say and bite my lip, feeling completely exposed.

He grabs my hand and shakes his head. "Sweetheart, you have nothing to apologize for. I was a fucking dumbass. I was hurt, and my pride overshadowed any reason. I realized how fucking stupid I was for proposing you and Henry to move in so soon, and I was scared that it's too late now after I treated you like that. I told myself that I'm too busy with my company to deal with that, but in reality I was petrified that you will tell me to beat it. As you have the right to do still." Then he glances in the direction of the front door with a shameful grimace and adds. "And I'm sorry about today. You showed up looking like that... And you're so goddamn sexy when you're angry. I just lost my mind completely."

I smooth the material of the dress on my lap, feeling my cheeks redden. "I sort of, got the dress for you," I mutter and feel like I want the earth to swallow me whole having admitted that.

"Did you?" Brody smiles with satisfaction and eyes my cleavage briefly. "Well, if you wanted to bring me to my knees, I happily own up to the fact that I was fucking crushed the second I lay my eyes on you."

"So, uh..." I say shakily, changing back to the subject. "You said that you won't press on the matter of us living here. But, umm, does it mean that's not something that you want anymore?" I ask timidly and peer at Brody from under my lashes.

He straightens in his seat and throws me a questioning look.

"Because I think I would like to try... the relationship thing, I mean."

"Really?" Brody asks slowly, his face getting unreadable.

I lick my dry lips and take a breath before I reply with conviction. "Yes. Damon Brody, if we were to recreate the scene from last week, my answer now would be yes."

I watch with a frown as he stands up from the table without a word, his face determined, then marches to my chair and pulls me up by the arms before throwing me over the shoulder.

"Brody, what the fuck are you doing?" I scream in bewilderment.

"You said if we were to recreate the scene, you would say yes this time. I say, let's go and recreate it," he responds, and I laugh.

"You're crazy! Let me go!" I plead, but I can't stop the giant grin from appearing on my face.

"Not in a million years," he says as he carries me to the bathroom.

206

CHAPTER XIV

T *hree months later*

"Bye, Gary, thank you for everything. Take care," I say and hug my, as of today, former employer.

"You too, Jenny, don't be a stranger. All right? And tell that man of yours he better take good care of you, or he's going to have my fists to answer to," the man says playfully.

I chuckle and step back from his embrace. "I'll tell him." Then I check the time, and groan, "Shoot, I need to go. I'm still not packed, and I need to pick up Henry from his grandmother."

"I thought Brody's aunt is babysitting Henry," Gary remarks as he walks me to my car.

I sigh and open the door. "Brody and I have been on the fence over the subject, to be honest. He thinks we shouldn't leave Henry with Rita anymore because she's not suitable for the role of a nanny, and that it's better for him to stay with Ruth when I'm at work."

The older man hums in his throat and asks, "What do you think?"

"I know he's right, but Henry loves Rita, and I don't want to subject him to so many changes in so little time. I mean, it's been only three months since we moved in with Brody, and he's getting pretty well-adjusted, but he misses the old hag."

"Well, I'm sure you're going to figure it out. But what I've come to learn in my own marriage after thirty plus years, is that there's no better way to solve disputes than with a compromise." Gary smiles and taps me on my shoulder.

"Yeah, I guess," I say and scratch behind my ear. "Anyway, I better hit the road."

We say our goodbyes one more time, and then after I get in and put the car in gear, I dial Brody's number before putting it on the speaker.

As predicted, the voicemail picks up, so I leave a message, "Hey, babe. Just left Gary's, and I'm heading over to Rita's to get our little rascal. I know you're busy with work, so call me when you're on your way. I can't wait for our first holidays together. Okay, bye."

I smile to myself and think about how happy I've been lately. Things have been running smoothly between me and Brody since we decided to live together. After the first week, I couldn't even remember the reason I was so scared to make the next move. I can't imagine my life now without Brody in it.

Since it took a lot of hustle to drive between our place, Gary's, and Rita's house, and to make time for ourselves in between, I decided to look for a new job somewhere closer.

At the encouragement from Brody, I enlisted in some online courses to get my GED, and with a little help from Mark, I got a part-time position as a receptionist in the medical center. These were all big steps for me, but with the support of my wonderful man, and my new family, I feel like I can conquer anything life throws at me.

Since Brody's schedule got a little looser next week, and it won't be until next month that I start my new job, we decided to go on a little vacation to the West Coast.

I have never been anywhere further than Madison in my life, so to say that I'm super excited to see the sea would be putting it mildly.

With that in mind, I sing along with the radio as I park in front of Rita's house.

I turn off the engine, get out and then come into Rita's house without knocking.

"Hey, I'm a little earlier today because we want to..." I start to say as I breeze into the living room, where I know I'll find the old grumpy woman. I stop in my tracks, however, when I realize there's someone else in the room.

"Ricky?" I ask surprised and then address Rita, feeling the anger spike in me. "I thought I made myself clear about this. The court will decide if he's allowed to see Henry."

"Little Jenny." Ricky smiles jovially and opens his arms as if he's expecting me to greet him with a hug. "Is this how you greet your man who's just got out of prison? The father of your child? Come on, you know better than that."

I shake my head and refrain from rolling my eyes at him. "You are not my man, and you're not supposed to be around Henry until the court approves. I don't know what you two are trying to achieve here, but the judge will be hearing about this. And we're leaving. Where's Henry?"

"I have him right here," I hear a raspy voice behind, and I whirl around only to take a wobbly step back.

"No," I whisper brokenly and look at the man who still features in my nightmares. The man that almost ruined me. The man who killed my mother.

"It's you." I feel the blood drain from my face, as I eye the monster that is so different from the respectable sheriff he used to be. Yet, the coldness in his eyes couldn't be mistaken for someone else's. His greasy hair is almost to his shoulders, half of his face is obscured by a badly trimmed beard, and his skin looks ashy and unhealthy. Other than that, he's in desperate need of new clothes. The shirt he's wearing looks like it used to be white but now is brownish with ugly-looking stains, and the jeans he's wearing have more holes in them than Swiss cheese.

My eyes zero in on the toddler he's holding, and I think I'm moments from my heart jumping out of my chest at the horrifying sight. I blink slowly, hoping for the image to change, but after I reopen my eyes, there's no such luck. This is my worst nightmare playing out live right in front of me.

"No. Henry," I say and try to reach out to take him but stop when my father lifts the bottom of his shirt to show me the gun he has tucked into his pants.

"No-uh, Jennifer. Behave. We wouldn't want anything awful happening to this cute little baby of yours." My father smiles, revealing his yellowed teeth.

"Wh-why are you here? What do you w-want?" I ask, hardly getting the words out because of the fear literally choking me.

He laughs, but there's nothing humorous about the sound. I feel the goosebumps arising on my skin. "To meet my grandson, of course! I've been hearing so much about the little squirt, I just couldn't wait to see him in person."

I glance at Henry, who seems to get a little agitated by the fact that I haven't made a move to greet him yet, as I always do. He kicks his little legs out, indicating that he wants to be let down on the floor.

If David feels that, he doesn't show it, as he continues to look at me with a predatory smile, holding Henry in a tight grip.

"How did you find me? Find us?" I ask to buy myself some time to think of a way to get my child out of here.

I glance at Rita, hoping for any help, but find her looking away as she sits in her armchair stiffly. The only indicator that she knows something is very wrong is the way her bony hands bite into the armrests. When I glance at Ricky, he's lighting up a cigarette watching the scene in front of him like he would be watching a very dull soap opera and not his own son being in danger.

I search around for anything I could use as a weapon as David starts to talk, seemingly enjoying the situation. "You know, I didn't think I would find you. Thought you'll be smarter, and get far from here. But I always knew you're dumber than a box of rocks. Anyway, I was keeping an eye on that motherfucker who ruined everything, and imagine my surprise when suddenly you came into the picture. How delightful, that the wonder couple reunited," he finishes sarcastically, and I hear Ricky snort indignantly.

"So, what's the big plan here? You're going to kill me in daylight, like you killed Mom, and then what?" I ask.

"Your mom." He frowns and shakes his head as if he's trying to sweep away his intrusive thoughts. "Your mom was a whore, and she was disobedient. I had no choice, no choice," he says quietly as if he's trying to convince himself.

Jesus Christ, he's completely fucking nuts.

"As for the plan, just wait and see, Jennifer. Just wait and see, it's going to be epic," he states proudly and takes the gun out. I take a step back and gasp. "Boy, take the kid," he commands Ricky and then points the gun at me. "We're going for a ride."

211

• • • •

AS SOON AS THE BAG gets pulled from my head, I take a deep breath and immediately find out what a bad idea that was when the dusty air fills my lungs and I start coughing uncontrollably.

I look up from the wooden floor I've been dumped on, with bleary eyes when I feel a hand rubbing me on the back. "There, there, little Jenny. You're fine."

"Where's Henry?" I croak and look around the devastated room in a desperate search for my boy. "Ricky, where is he?"

"Calm down. Damn it, you really think I would put my own kid in harm's way?" he asks angrily.

"You already did! You motherfucker!" I hiss and try to move, but remember my hands are tied behind my back. "I swear to fucking God, Ricky, if there's so much as one hair out of place on Henry's head, I will scalp you myself, and then chop your useless body into tiny pieces before I feed it to wild animals."

"You were always cute when you're angry." He laughs and stands up before me. "But stop being so dramatic. Nothing will happen to you two. The kid fell asleep on the way here, so I left him in the car."

When he sees my horrified expression, he lifts his hand. "I left the window open. Jesus Christ, you make me look like an idiot."

"Maybe because you are one," I say angrily and survey the open space, surprised to realize they have brought me back to Bell Ridge, and to the fucking Mill of all places. The interior looks even worse now, but I've been here enough times in my teenage years to recognize it right off the bat.

I don't see a sign of my father being close, so I hiss at Ricky, "Untie me, you fucking dick, before David comes back."

"You know what, your father was right. You do have a big mouth and no respect for the men in your life. I can see that now myself. We do need to teach you a fucking lesson. Same with that asshole you've been playing house with while I was rotting away in prison."

"You're so full of shit. Let me go. I don't know what that psycho told you or promised you to get on board with this crazy idea, but you need to stop it right now. I mean it, Ricky, you have no idea how dangerous he is," I try to reason with him, but the stubborn set of his jaw already tells me I'm getting nowhere.

Deciding to change my tactics, I soften my voice. "Please, Ricky. We can still work it out between us. We could co-parent and stuff. I can forget all this happened as long as you get us the fuck out of here."

Ricky opens his mouth to answer me, but just then my father decides to join us. If possible, he looks even more disheveled than before and is carrying a shotgun under his arm. He mutters to himself and goes straight to the graffiti-covered window to look at the surroundings.

"It won't be long now. It won't be long," he repeats over and over again.

"Ricky," I whisper. "Look at him, he's batshit crazy. Get us out before it's too late."

This time, I can see the doubt set in Ricky's eyes, as he looks between me and my father.

"Whatever he told you, it's not real. He's a psychopath. I don't know his plan, but it will not end well for any of us..." I continue and jump in place when my father suddenly comes closer.

"What the fuck are you two whispering about?" He positions the shotgun, so it points straight at Ricky's chest. "Don't you listen to that viper, boy."

My ex-boyfriend's eyebrows lift as he steps back. "I wasn't, sir. We were just catching up." His tone is casual, but I notice the way his fist clenches at his sides. Oh yeah, now he's starting to get it. Fucking moron.

"Catching up? Sounds like a good idea, I would love to catch up with you, Jennifer," the homeless-looking man crouches in front of me and licks his lips. "So, what have you been up to, other than dicking around with that massive idiot Brody?"

"Not much. But I see you've been busy with dressing like a hobo and killing innocent fucking women," I grind out, and then spit in his face.

My father brings his hand to his dirty face and wipes the moisture slowly before he casually backhands me. My head snaps to the side, and I groan.

"Hey, you told me you won't harm her," Ricky protests, and tries to come closer. Once again, he's stopped when my father points the barrel of the gun straight at him.

"You don't give orders here. Now, make yourself useful and stay on the lookout. I want to know when that piece of shit gets here to save the damsel in distress," David commands, and then lifts the weapon higher when Ricky stays put, looking conflicted. "Don't make me tell you twice."

214

Ricky lifts his hands in surrender and nods. Before he can turn, my father looks around as if suddenly remembering something. "Where's the little kid?"

Without missing a beat, Ricky states, "I left him upstairs, like you told me. He's sleeping."

I frown at the blatant lie but don't comment, glad that Henry's not in the direct line of danger just yet. At least if I can believe a word from his bastard father's mouth. I put it aside for now because I can't think about it if I'm to somehow get out of the Mill alive. I won't be able to help my child if I'm trapped in this shithole.

Concentrating back on my father, I decide to engage him in a conversation, after all, the fucker always liked the sound of his own voice. "So, what's up with this new look, daddy?"

My father glances back at me and smiles, before tugging on the hem of the stained shirt. "You like? Turns out I found the perfect camouflage. I can't count all the times I've had a police cruiser pass me by, supposedly in search for me." He downright giggles with delight. "Dress as a homeless person and boom, you're invisible. It works like a charm. It's as if people have it engraved in them to look away."

"Wow, brilliant," I respond with fake admiration as I slap my hands behind searching for anything sharp, like a nail or something protruding from the uneven, old floors to cut the ropes on my wrists. "So, was this before or after you murdered your wife?"

"Marissa was a whore!" he roars suddenly, startling me. "She didn't obey me. She was unfaithful. And she was a lying bitch to her last breath." He steps back and laughs maniacally. "I always felt it. I did. I never loved you like a father should love his own flesh and blood. I didn't, I didn't..." He looks away and scratches at his beard.

"You're delusional," I mutter, but David doesn't seem to hear me.

"We were all friends, back in the day. All together. Brothers until death, they said. All liars. All..." He looks back at me and studies my face with an almost tender expression. "I can see him in you now. I couldn't see myself in you. I felt that. Somehow I always knew."

"What the fuck are you talking about? See who?" I ask with a frown.

"Robert. My friend. My brother." He cackles again, making me startle one more time, and I quickly glance at Ricky, then point my eyes at the door, and raise my eyebrows. "You can imagine my surprise when he proudly showed me the photo of his daughter, and she looked just like you when you were younger." I snap my head to gape at David.

When he sees the shock on my face, he smirks. "I knew he would never own up to that. No man with half of a brain would want you. You were always useless. Well... maybe we can rectify that still."

Before I can register what's happening, he pulls my legs toward him and grabs the hem of my jeans, trying to shove his disgusting hands inside. I scream bloody murder and try to kick him away.

"What the fuck, man? What the hell are you doing?" Ricky screams and throws the older man off me. He's breathing sharply and looking at my attacker incredulously before he shakes his head. "Nah, man. I'm done here. I'm calling the fucking cops." He turns around toward the door.

Before Ricky can make even two steps, however, the deafening sound of a gun going off resonates through the walls, and I watch in slow motion as the back of his head explodes. The time then fast-forwards and his body falls to the ground like a sack of potatoes with a gaping hole the size of a fist in his skull.

"No!" I cry and start thrashing around. "No! Ricky! No, no, no..." I cry, unable to move my eyes from his lifeless body.

The man I considered my father just a few minutes ago, steps into my line of sight and mutters. "Don't act so surprised. Nobody was going to get out of here alive anyway."

CHAPTER XV

Brody

"I already talked to the supplier, and everything should be delivered by the end of the week, but if there's a problem you can call," I say to the site manager as I pack my tools. I'm eager to finish for the day, and I was supposed to be done for the day an hour ago, but the problems seem to be popping up like mushrooms when you're on your last day before the holiday.

"Hey, boss!" a young laborer named Tom calls me.

I turn around with a sigh and impatiently yell out, "What is it now?"

The shy boy looks abashed at my tone and slows his steps, making me feel like an asshole, so I lower my voice and ask calmly, "What is it, Tommy? I was just on my way out."

He rubs his neck, looking doubtful. "No it's nothing, boss, but I was just on my break, and you left your things there." Tom points with his thumb to the bench the workers are using to eat lunch together. "I was going to ignore it, but your phone called like five times in a row, so I thought it might be important..."

I frown in the direction of my things, then clap the boy on the shoulder with a muttered "Thanks," and march through the construction.

I don't carry my phone with me during work because very often I'm unable to hear or answer it anyway. I do get plenty of phone calls as a business owner, but five in a row makes me instantly feel apprehensive.

As I get to my bag, the phone starts ringing, and I frown when I see that it's a call from Robert.

"Brody," I grunt out, holding the phone between my ear and shoulder as I start to collect my things and then head toward my car.

"Hey, man. I'm glad I caught you," the detective greets me casually, but I am right away able to pick up on the tension in his voice.

"What's up, man?"

"So, there's been... um, development in the case. I'm calling to warn you," Robert starts, then exhales loudly into the receiver. "I've been keeping an eye on that Ricky guy that Jenny used to... date, and, um..."

"Ricky?" I ask, as I get behind the wheel and slam the doors. "What's he to you?"

"Um, you know... I'm just keeping an eye out for her. You know, just doing my job," he responds, but I can tell he's full of shit.

"I knew he had a big chance of getting out, so I started to look into him a few months ago... You know, the basic stuff, what's he up to, will he cause problems for Jennifer and Henry..."

I hum in my throat, and start the car. "That's all great, Rob. But will you get to the fucking point or what?"

"Yeah, sorry. So, I didn't find much. The guy is pretty much an idiot, and he seems harmless enough. But three months ago, he started to get regular visits, and calls from someone. For a year, he only had like two people visiting him, so I thought it odd."

"So, what? It was probably a lawyer discussing his parole hearing or some other shit," I say, getting irked with the subject.

"Not a lawyer. A person looking very similar to David Wallace," Robert states, and I almost swerve to the side.

"You're fucking joking."

"I didn't confirm it yet. The guy used a fake name, and a fake ID for the visits, and he was calling the prison from a number that is already disconnected. I got my answer when I saw the footage of the meetings, and he looks different, but I would recognize that man even in the deepest depths of hell," Robert says with conviction and I pull off the road, unable to concentrate on where I'm going.

Self-consciously, I rub at the burned half of my chest, and breathe through my nose. "What the fuck is he playing at?" I mutter, almost to myself.

"If he's got to that Ricky fella, it can't be anything good. That's why I'm telling you this. So, you can keep an eye out. It would be best if you and Jenny lay low for a while until I'm able to learn more about his possible whereabouts."

"We were leaving town anyway for a while. When did you find out all this?" I ask, and feel the panic arising in me.

"I called you right away after seeing the footage," Robert responds. "Where's Jenny? She shouldn't be on her own, especially since Ricky got out last week."

"Shit. I didn't know he's out," I say angrily. "Hey, did you try calling me before about this?"

"Um, no. This is the first time I'm calling? What's with you?" Robert asks, just as a notification pops up about an incoming call from Jen.

"I'll call you back, I have another call," I grunt, and disconnect before he can say a word.

"Hey, sweetheart," I answer, trying to sound calm.

Every muscle in my body locks, however, when I don't hear Jenny's sweet voice but a broken raspy whisper in between sobs.

"I'm sorry, so sorry. I didn't... I didn't know..."

"Who is this?" I can barely get the words out.

"It's R-Rita," the woman sniffles. "They took them," she whispers and starts crying.

"Who took whom?" I almost yell into the phone, but all I get is the sound of a wail. "Damn it, woman. Why do you have Jenny's phone?"

"The man, and my Ricky. They took them, and I-I let them. Oh, God!... I'll never forgive myself," she says, and I hear rustling paper. "The man... he t-told me to give you a message. It says 'come to the old farm, if you c-call the police, I will bl-blow her f-fucking brains out.'" The old woman then starts to sob uncontrollably, so I slowly lower the phone from my ear and disconnect.

I swallow painfully, and stare at my shaking hands. I thought I already faced my greatest fear in life, and that I lived through hell. I was a Marine, and I saw people dying on a mission. When I was in the FBI, I saw some despicable crimes. The last time I faced David Wallace, I almost lost my own life.

But I never felt this terror fueled rage inside of me. I never felt the need to burn the entire world to the ground just to get to the people I love.

In a matter of seconds, my breathing slows down, and my senses sharpen when I realize where he's keeping Jen and Henry.

I reach into the glove box, where I keep my gun, and check if it's loaded. Then, I call Robert back.

"Hey, can I trust you?" I ask as soon as I hear his voice on the other side.

. . . .

"I THOUGHT I MADE MYSELF clear," I growl, as soon as Robert gets out of his car with a young-looking police officer trailing right behind him. "What about you coming here alone did you not get?"

We are on the outskirts of Bell Ridge, right at the fork of the road, with one way leading into town and the other going straight to the Mill.

"Calm down, Damon. We don't know what awaits us there. But what we do know is that it's a trap. Officer Rusoe will stay behind unless we need a backup," Robert says patiently, then glances at the road. "How far from here is the house?"

I eye the detective with a grimace, then focus on the task. "We have about half a mile to go. I reckon to get the slightest element of surprise, we move along the tree line so that we see the place from afar while staying hidden in the shadows. However, if the place is like I remember, there won't be a way to get inside without him noticing if he's on a lookout. So, as soon as we're out of the woods, we move fast. I go in the front, and you, Rob, will go around the property to get inside from the back. You." I point at the pale policeman. "Stay back and don't engage unless I say so or unless everything turns to shit. Then you run and call for the reinforcements. Got it?" The man nods, visibly shaken.

"I think I missed the part where we made you the boss, Brody," Robert sneers and steps toward me.

Without thinking, I grab him by the collar of his shirt and slam him to the side of his car.

"Shut the fuck up, man! Don't make me regret calling you. This isn't the time for you to play the big detective. This is about saving the woman that I love!" I hiss into his face.

"And it's about saving my daughter, so I just want to make sure the plan is solid," Robert replies calmly, looking unfazed by my sudden display of aggression.

I drop my hands and step back from the shorter man. "Daughter? The fuck are you talking about?"

He looks to the side, and his jaw ticks before he peers back at my face. "Jennifer is my daughter. I suspected..." He pauses to rub his mouth before continuing. "I suspected she could be mine when Marissa became pregnant, but after our ways parted, it was easier for me to accept her lie and move on. She looked... happy with David."

"When did you find out?" I ask in a low voice.

Robert's face gets a little pink before he responds shamefully. "Ever since I took the case from you three years ago. One look at her file photo, and I just knew..."

"Jesus Christ, and you didn't say anything? What the..." I mutter, trying to digest the news, but then shake my head and stand straighter. "It doesn't matter, the time is running out. Instead of chitchatting about your shitty life choices, we need to get a move on before that maniac does something to her or to Henry."

"You're right," Robert agrees and addresses the young cop. "Rusoe, are you ready?"

"Yes, sir," he answers right away, looking a little more sure of himself now.

We move through the forest, stopping every once in a while to listen for any unusual sounds, but the area seems quiet, with only the birds singing accompanying the rustle of fallen leaves crashing under our boots.

When we come close to the clearing, we get an unobscured view of the ruined house, the dilapidated barn, and acres of outgrown grass. The only indication of anyone being here is Jen's car parked less than fifty feet from us, at the end of the area that used to be the driveway.

"Okay, this is the place. Rob, on my mark, run to the back entrance. Keep your head as low as you can. I will get through the front and try to divert his attention to me, so you can grab Jen and the kid when possible. Rusoe, you stay back, and if you hear shots being fired, make the call. Hopefully, we can do this without any bloodshed..." The moment I say this, I hear the sound of a gunfire inside the house.

"No! Ricky!" I whirl around at the loud cry, recognizing Jen's voice, and almost jump into a sprint when Robert's hand stops me.

"Wait, do you hear that? In the car..." he hisses into my ear, and I realize what he means. The sound of a baby calling for his mom reaches me, and I know it could only be Henry.

I bend at the waist and start crawling toward the vehicle, hoping the grass covers me at least a little. Then I open the car door, and exhale in relief when I see the baby looking at me with big eyes.

"Hey, little guy," I whisper, and unclasp him from the car seat.

"Hi." Henry smiles adoringly, and then looks around. "Where is mommy?"

"We're going to get your mom real soon, but for now, I need you to stay quiet and hold on to me very tight. You think you can do that?" I ask with a smile, trying not to spook him.

The kid nods and extends his short arms to curl them around my neck. I look toward the two men still waiting behind the trees, and when I get a confirmation that they got us covered, I move swiftly through the grass with Henry grasping onto me like a little monkey.

As soon as we're in the clear, I hand the toddler into Rusoe's arms. "Change of plans, take the kid as far away from here as possible. And make the call on your way," I start to turn but when I see the cop standing still with Henry, and looking unsure, I hiss, "Fucking go!"

The young man snaps into action, and I grab Robert by the arm. "The rest of the plan stays the same, let's go."

I run toward the house, without checking if Robert is also on the move, and take my gun out before pausing right outside the door.

My first instinct is to kick it right off its hinges, and go in gun blazing, but I know I need to calm my breathing and wait until Robert has a chance to get into the position.

Timing is key in a situation like this, I tell myself, and count to ten, all the time listening for more sounds coming out of the house, but it's eerily quiet.

There hasn't been a second gunshot, and I know that was Jen's voice that I was hearing before. It's only been two minutes, so she has to be alive.

She can't be dead. She's going to be all right. I just gotta keep my cool, and...

I kick the door, and walk in holding my gun raised, and yell, "Wallace!" I check the first two rooms but find them empty before I hear a frightened voice calling.

"Get out, Brody! Please run," Jen begs from somewhere, and it's the first time I hear her sounding so scared.

I almost trip over something in the dark corridor, and look down, only to realize that it's a dead body. The man had the half of his head blown off, but his face seems untouched, with a look of shock forever engraved on it.

I lift my head when I see movement, but quickly lower the gun when I recognize Robert lurking in the shadows.

He gestures around to indicate that he checked the other rooms, and that they have to be in the one in front of us. I nod, and raise my hand for him to stay put on the other side of the doorway before I slowly turn the knob.

My nostrils flare, when I see what awaits me inside. Jenny kneels in the middle of the room, stripped to her underwear, with her hands clasped in front of her. On her left side there are pieces of a cut rope, and what's left of her clothes. Behind her stands a ragged looking man with a rifle.

When the door creaks, she lifts her head, and one tear escapes her eye.

"No..." she says sadly. "No, please..."

I point the gun straight at David's head, and seethe, "Let her go."

"And what if I don't want to do that?" Wallace laughs maliciously, not making any attempts to raise his arms.

I reposition my hands on the gun, and repeat more forcefully, "Let. Her. Go. Let her go or I'll shoot."

"Nah, I wouldn't do that if I were you." He smiles, and I frown when Jen starts to sob. When I look back up, though, I get why.

David opens his unbuttoned shirt to reveal explosives strapped to his chest, then he lifts his hand to present a small device with a button.

"I thought it would give us a little more time to talk before your hotheadedness causes more inconveniences for us. Come on in, don't be shy." He waves his hand indicating a place on the floor next to Jenny.

"The moment I'm on him, you grab her and go," I catch Robert saying from somewhere close, his words are barely audible.

I nod, making it seem like I'm responding to Wallace's command, and put the gun away by the door before stepping fully into the room.

Purposefully, I'm moving further than he pointed, forcing him to turn his head a little in order to see me, in the hope it gives Robert a chance to sneak in.

The maniac doesn't even notice, happy with the sight of me kneeling in front of him. I see the detective moving with the corner of my eye, so to cover the sounds of wood creaking under his feet, I decide to distract the crazy man hovering above me.

"So, this is what you need to do to feel important or relevant? Kidnap a woman and a defenseless child, then shoot a man behind his back?" I taunt, not even thinking about what I'm saying, and ignoring the sounds of Jen's weeps. I just need to rile him up enough for him to drop his guard. "By the way, what did you promise to the idiot to get him on board with your crazy ass plan?"

Wallace throws his head back and laughs. "Man, that poor bastard. It was too easy, too fucking easy." He shakes his head with a gleeful smile. "Can you believe that he actually thought I will help him 'persuade Jennifer to come back to him'?" He makes the quote marks with his fingers, and I eye the detonator in his palm.

"Yeah, that's hilarious. You're the man," I deadpan, and try not to react when I see Robert's shadow in my peripheral. "A man who's got nothing because you destroyed everything good you had going on in your life. And now you are just a shadow. A fucking husk of a person you wanted so persistently to be. No one will remember you, no one will mourn your death..." I tell him gravelly, and slowly stand up.

"No! Stay the fuck down! We're not done!" David yells with his eyes bulged in fury. He pockets the detonator and makes a move to get his rifle, but before he can reach it, a body slams to his side, making them both drop to the floor.

"Go!" Robert screams, as he fumbles with the enemy.

I quickly grab Jen into my arms, and run toward the front door. We're barely making it past the small porch, when the force of the exploding bomb throws us away. Instinctively, I curl my body around Jenny's when I feel the heat of a fire touching my back, and the shards of glass flying everywhere. We land on the grass, with me on top, when I feel something slamming into the back of my thigh.

I yell out in pain but stay in my position until I feel it's safe to lift my head. My ears are ringing, and my sight grows dim, but all I can focus on is the frail body under me.

Her eyes are shut tight, and she's breathing very fast, so I lift my shaking hand to her face.

"Jen, please, tell me that you're all right," I beg her, aware of the fact I'm slurring my words.

"Yes, I think I am," she answers and her eyes spring open. As soon as she focuses on me, her face pinches in worry. "Brody?"

I slide to the side, feeling like I've got no control over my limbs, and land ungracefully facing the ground. I feel my body being repositioned, so I lie on my back facing the sky. I can't comprehend the sounds or movements around me as I blink slowly at the delicate cloud above me.

Then her face appears, backlit by the sunshine, making her look like an angel. The only thing wrong with the scenario are the tears streaming down from her widened eyes.

"I love you so much," I mutter, but I'm not even sure I know how to pronounce words anymore.

"No, no, no, where is all this blood coming from?" Jen asks frantically, and her face disappears for a moment before I hear a loud curse. She comes back into the view, and I try to lift my hand, so I could touch her soft skin one more time before I go.

"Everything will be okay now." I want to smile, yet I am unable to tell if my face is listening to my brain's commands. "You are safe, and Henry is safe..." My eyes close involuntarily.

"No, please, Brody. Don't leave me. Please, I love you. Please don't leave me. Don't let go. Fight for me, please,

please...Don't give up," her distraught voice turns more, and more distant as I start feeling lighter, and lighter.

I slowly go to a place where my body no longer exists, and I'm at peace, slipping into the black abyss.

Epilogue

Jenny - 1 year later

I wake up with a gasp, and look at my hands, expecting to see blood streaming between my fingers. When all I see is ivory skin illuminated by the stream of morning light, I breathe in relief, realizing that it was just another nightmare. Or more like a memory when it comes to those kinds of dreams I've been having.

I turn my head to the side and frown at the empty, cold place next to me. With a sigh, I sit down and lower my legs to the cold floor. The sensation takes me back in time for a moment, and I glare at the harsh surface.

"What the fuck?" I mutter, feeling unsettled. I get to my feet with a groan, and step out of the bedroom, to check on Henry.

When I see that his bed is empty, I peek into the bathroom, only to realize that it's empty too. I instantly feel my blood pressure rising.

"Henry?" I call, and my voice echoes around the house, but no answer follows.

I move to the staircase and descend carefully, realizing that it's even colder downstairs.

"Are you here?" I ask, and look around, feeling my heartbeat increase with each passing second of silence.

"Calm down," I berate myself under my breath, but it does nothing to halt my rising panic as I search through the kitchen and living room, and find the whole house vacant.

"No. Where are you?" I mutter and tug on my hair, looking frantically around. "This can't be happening."

Blinded by the fear, I go barefoot through the back sliding door to step on the newly built, but unfinished, terrace, searching for Henry. Logically, I know, he couldn't reach the doorknob to let himself outside, but still, I survey the quiet area around the house, and call for him again.

Now, almost fully swallowed by the need to find my missing child, I reach out my hand toward the railing, and try to walk down the half-built staircase frame, when I register a sharp pain in my right hand.

I look down in shock at the protruding nail that pierced my skin, then wail in distress, when I see a single stream of blood flowing down my palm and onto my fingers, before it drops onto the fresh wood.

Just like in my dream. Just like that day when...

I'm not even sure when I collapsed onto the cold wooden boards, but the fog starts to slowly clear from my mind as I stare at my bleeding hand, when the familiar sound of a cane tapping on the floor reaches my ear.

"Sweetheart?" Brody calls from the house.

"Here..." I say, but it comes out raspy and weak, so, I take a deep breath and say louder. "I'm here."

The sound of the cane gets closer, before I hear the sliding door open, and Brody joins me on the terrace.

"Jen! What happened?" He walks closer and immediately pulls me up from the boards to carry me back inside, his walking stick dropping to the floor in the process.

"Your leg," I mutter worriedly, as Brody steps quickly through the door.

"Mommy?" an uncertain voice reaches me from somewhere below.

I open my mouth to respond, but Brody beats me to it. "Mommy is fine, little man. Go upstairs and play, all right? Just remember to hold on to that banister as you climb the stairs."

"Okay, Daddy," Henry calls, the thumping of his little feet confirming he's doing just that.

I'm being gently placed on the couch, before Brody kneels in front of me and grabs my hand to get a closer look.

"What the hell happened? Why did you go out there? I told you it's not safe for you or Henry to go to the terrace just yet," Brody says, his eyebrows pulled together in worry.

"I..." I swallow hard, avoiding his eyes. "I thought you're at work. I got up to get Henry, and he wasn't there. The floor was cold, and I don't know. I just started to panic, and went out to look for him. I wasn't careful, I..."

"Hey, Jen, baby." When I still don't look at him, he touches my face and turns it so that I can't evade his gaze. "I'm sorry. The heating broke down during the night. And there was no hot water. You were sleeping, and I wanted to avoid waking you since you were having such a rough time lately with this little one." He points to my slightly rounded stomach, and smiles tenderly before sobering. "I called the guys at work that I will be in later, and went out to buy some parts I needed. Henry came with me, so he wouldn't be running around on his own as you rest. I honestly thought you wouldn't even know we were gone. I'm sorry it scared you."

"Oh my God," I whisper and look down in shame before the tears come unwillingly. "I'm losing my goddamn mind, Brody. I'm so fucked up."

"Sweetheart, no." Brody sits next to me and takes me into his arms, which, of course, makes me cry harder. "You're fine. We're all fine."

"I'm so tired of being like this. I mean... It's been a year since I almost lost you. Both of you. I'm scared this life we're building here is going to be taken away from us in a blink of an eye."

"Jen, I wholeheartedly understand. But you need to realize that your father is gone. There's no imminent danger lurking around anymore. We survived him, we can survive everything else life throws at us, and we'll do it together. Came all this way, didn't we?" Brody smiles warmly and squeezes my shoulder, before he gets up and helps me to my feet. "Now, let's clean that wound."

Before he can lead me to the bathroom, I tug on his sleeve when I notice his limp. "Wait, your cane. It stayed outside."

Brody waves his hand dismissively. "I'll go get it later. It's not like I can't walk."

We go in, and Brody grabs my hips to put me on the bathroom counter next to the sink, where, I'm pretty sure, we've made the new addition growing in my stomach a few months back.

My thoughts must have been written on my face because Brody chuckles with a teasing gleam in his eyes. "Taking a walk down the memory lane?"

When my face heats, and I roll my eyes, he smirks, "I'll take that as a yes. Okay, what do we have here?"

Brody clears the cut on my palm and puts on a bandage on it, after which he gives me a kiss. "Do you remember what you said to me when I was bleeding out to death?"

"Don't you fucking die on me?" I ask humorlessly.

One corner of Brody's lips twitches before he shakes his head. "No, smart ass. You told me to not let go. You asked me to fight for you. And I did. Always." He moves closer, so our foreheads touch. "I'm going to fight for you until my last dying breath, Jen." He promises with conviction, and my eyes once again fill up with tears.

Those goddamn pregnancy hormones. And that goddamn beautiful, awesome, incredible, out of this world man.

"God damn you, Damon Brody. You made me cry again," I grumble, and give him a peck on the cheek. "But I love you."

"I love you too, sweetheart," he murmurs, then straightens and helps me down. "Now, I would love to recreate some of those fond memories right now, but I'm sure Henry will be searching for you soon, and I do need to fix that heater."

I grin and move past him to open the door, just as our son screams from upstairs, "Mommy!"

We both start laughing, and I yell back, "I'm coming, Henry!"

"You'll be coming tonight, all right," Brody says quietly, and then dodges my hand as I try to swipe at him playfully. He limps out of the room to retrieve his cane from the terrace, and I go to the staircase.

Just when I put my foot on the first step, the doorbell rings.

"Will you get that?" Brody calls.

I look down at Brody's old t-shirt and the overstretched leggings I use as pajamas since I gained weight, and frown.

"I'll get it," I answer him, and then yell, "Just a minute!" When the doorbell rings again.

I move to the door, and look through the peephole, but only get the view of the back of a woman's head.

Cranking the door open just a little, I ask the twitchy person on our front porch, "Can I help you?"

Then she turns, and I let out a yelp of surprise as I let go of the door.

"Claire?" I ask with eyes wide open, looking at my former best friend. When I notice the state she's in, I take a step back, and frown.

Claire steps from foot to foot, not meeting my eyes, and mutters. "I'm sorry for showing up like this. But I need help."

THE END

Ingram Content Group UK Ltd.
Milton Keynes UK
UKHW010809190623
423681UK00016B/765